Jet Set Docs

How far will they go to find the one they love?

Introducing this season's hottest Harlequin Medical Romance novels packed with your summertime dose of dreamy doctors, pulse-racing drama and sizzling romantic tension! Fly up, up and away and follow these globe-trotting docs as they travel to stunning international destinations for work...but end up finding a special someone in their arms!

Grab your passport and find out in

Second Chance in Santiago by Tina Beckett
One Night to Sydney Wedding by JC Harroway
The Doctor's Italian Escape by Annie Claydon
Spanish Doc to Heal Her by Karin Baine
ER Doc's South Pole Reunion by Juliette Hyland
Their Accidental Vegas Vows by Amy Ruttan

All available now!

Dear Reader,

I loved writing this book! A hero and heroine who I adored, finding each other in the beautiful city of Rome. Sometimes I felt that the book was almost (but not quite) writing itself!

But things weren't so easy for Doctors Joe and Bel. In many ways they're opposites, brought up within a couple of miles of each other in London but in very different worlds. But they have one piece of common ground. When the clinic that Joe has founded is threatened, they'll both do whatever it takes to make sure it survives. If that means they both need to be honest and learn to trust each other, then they'll even do that.

It's a hard-fought battle for them both to realize that they're not just better together, but they're made for each other. And I can't tell you how relieved I am that they both finally gave in. Thank you for reading Joe and Bel's story!

Annie x

THE DOCTOR'S ITALIAN ESCAPE

ANNIE CLAYDON

Recycling programs for this product may not exist in your area.

ISBN-13: 978-1-335-94314-9

The Doctor's Italian Escape

Harlequin Enterprises ULC
22 Adelaide St. West, 41st Floor
Toronto, Ontario M5H 4E3, Canada
www.Harlequin.com

Printed in U.S.A.

Cursed with a poor sense of direction and a propensity to read, **Annie Claydon** spent much of her childhood lost in books. A degree in English literature followed by a career in computing didn't lead directly to her perfect job—writing romance for Harlequin—but she has no regrets in taking the scenic route. She lives in London, a city where getting lost can be a joy.

Books by Annie Claydon

Harlequin Medical Romance

The Doctor's Reunion to Remember
Risking It All for a Second Chance
From the Night Shift to Forever
Stranded with the Island Doctor
Snowbound by Her Off-Limits GP
Cinderella in the Surgeon's Castle
Children's Doc to Heal Her Heart
One Summer in Sydney
Healed by Her Rival Doc
Country Fling with the City Surgeon
Winning Over the Off-Limits Doctor
Neurosurgeon's IVF Mix-Up Miracle
The GP's Seaside Reunion

Visit the Author Profile page
at Harlequin.com for more titles.

Praise for
Annie Claydon

"A spellbinding contemporary medical romance that will keep readers riveted to the page, *Festive Fling with the Single Dad* is a highly enjoyable treat from Annie Claydon's immensely talented pen."

—*Goodreads*

CHAPTER ONE

SEVEN O'CLOCK in the morning. Dr Joe Dixon swallowed the last gulp from his reusable coffee cup and turned his face up towards the morning sun, which slanted across the pavement. People were already up and out, making the most of what promised to be a fine Saturday morning, and he could take a moment or two before finding his keys and opening the doors of the community medical clinic.

People-watching had always been something of a hobby of his. When he was a kid he'd watched the confusing hierarchy of people whose job it was to shape his future, with increasing diligence. He'd practically made a study of them, keeping coded notes and lists for future reference. The social workers and children's rights officers who probably wouldn't bend the rules to make things happen, and those who might. Those who might be persuaded to smile and talk to him and those who wouldn't be getting too involved…

Things were different now and he'd taken his own life in hand—along with the lives of others—he watched his patients as assiduously as he'd once wished he might be watched. He'd rejected London, taking his revenge for the string of abandonments that the city had meted out to him, and come to Rome. People-watching had served him well here, too, allowing him to settle into his role as a trauma doctor at the English-speaking hospital in Rome and then pour all of his free time and money into setting up a free clinic, which served those who were dealing with the long-term effects of life-changing illness or injury.

And on this fine morning people-watching was sending a pleasurable tingle up his spine. Dr Bel Trueman, whose smile currently decorated the list of recent arrivals that was pinned up on the doctors' noticeboard, had seen his own notice asking for volunteers to help at the clinic and used the email address printed at the bottom. Joe had replied, thanking her for her interest and saying he'd be at the clinic from eight in the morning on Saturday. She was welcome to pop in at any time that was convenient and he'd show her around. And now she'd just turned the corner at the end of the street, a full hour early, and everyone else had suddenly become invisible.

Joe leaned against the front door of the clinic

watching her carefully, which probably wasn't strictly necessary because the days when his future was controlled by others were long gone. He'd seen her at the hospital, even been introduced briefly, before they both had to hurry in different directions, and she'd seemed no different from the other doctors who were working in the Trauma Unit. Focused and professional, wearing the uniform of scrubs under a crisp white coat. But now she seemed to have a lot more in common with the gradually awakening life on the streets.

If she hadn't spent time in Italy before, then she was a quick learner. In London a white shirt and skinny jeans could be as neutral as anyone wanted them to be, but here in Rome, women were more likely to treat any outfit as a fashion statement. The way her shirt was folded and tucked at the waist made Bel look as if she'd be at home on a catwalk, and her soft leather pumps and matching tan handbag completed the ensemble. Her dark curls, which looked casual but were probably the result of a determined encounter with a hairdryer this morning, made it clear that she didn't consider the weekend an appropriate time for the more severe tied-back style he'd seen at the hospital.

Gorgeous. She looked gorgeous, and if Joe had been the kind of man to fall for a virtual stranger then he'd be falling right now for Bel. Instead, he watched her carefully, returning her smile when she caught sight of him.

'Salve.' The one word betrayed a fluency that Joe could only envy. After three years in Rome, his Italian was good but still marked him out as English here at the clinic, where Italian was usually spoken.

He nodded in reply. 'You're early.'

Bel shrugged, indicating the coffee shop across the street. 'Not really. I have a book with me and I can be as late as you like.'

Don't!

Don't offer to buy the coffee, and join her beneath the flapping sunshades, in an effort to get to know Bel on a personal level. Joe had tried to get to know foster families and carers too many times, and even the couple who'd taken him in when he was ten and given him the stability of a real family hadn't been able to rub that instinct out. He couldn't think of anything urgent he needed to do before the clinic opened at ten o'clock, but he was sure to find something to keep him busy.

He turned, unlocking the door. 'I'll see you later, then?'

Her smile made *later* seem far too far away. 'Anything wrong with now?'

'Nothing at all. Thanks for coming…'

* * *

Joe motioned Bel inside, while he drew up the shutters over the windows. When he joined her, she was looking around the reception area with obvious approval.

'This is nice. Welcoming...' Her fingers skimmed the leaf of a large flowering plant on the reception desk. 'Not so scarily antiseptic as the hospital.'

'We do different things. Our patients are in a different stage of recovery from those we see in the Trauma Unit.'

Bel nodded. 'That's why I volunteered. I want to see what happens to people after they leave the hospital and what challenges they face. I'm hoping it'll make me a better doctor.'

Joe reckoned it probably would. No one spent their free time volunteering at a place like this unless they wanted more for their patients. 'We're not short on challenges.'

Red rag to a bull. Bel's dark eyes flashed as she looked up at him. Her perfect proportions had made her seem taller at a distance, but now he towered over her. It gave him the oddest feeling of wanting to protect her, although Bel's confident manner made it very clear that she could protect herself.

'It's exactly what I want. Everyone's a volunteer here?'

'Yes, apart from Maria, our receptionist. She's here every evening during the week, and on Saturdays.'

She nodded. 'What made you set this place up?'

'I volunteered with a similar clinic, back in London. When I came to Rome…' He shrugged. 'There are exactly the same kinds of needs here, and I'm passionate about my job.' Joe reminded himself, in case he was tempted to forget, that his job was the one and only thing he dared to be passionate about.

Bel nodded. 'You're a Londoner? Which part?'

Joe had moved too many times to lay claim to any part of the city as home, apart from the small house in Chelsea where his adoptive parents had lived. He was ten when they'd first fostered him and they were in their fifties, but they'd seen straight through his bravado, and had given him his first taste of what it was like to be part of a family. When they'd died, four years ago, Chelsea had been added to the list of places he didn't go back to.

'I moved around a lot. I was a Chelsea Football Club supporter.'

She grinned. 'What a coincidence—I grew up in Chelsea. My mum and dad still live there.'

If that was an invitation to share, Joe would pass on it. Bel's accent betrayed traces of the more prosperous side of the borough, and he guessed that she'd grown up in a different world from the one he had. He changed the subject.

'Have you worked in Italy before?'

'No, but I've always wanted to. My mother's Italian, and we used to come here for holidays. The job at the hospital is a real opportunity for me but it doesn't give me the chance to use my Italian. I hear that the clinic's mostly Italian speaking?'

'Yes, that's right. We've recruited as many local doctors and therapists as we can, and they've become the backbone of our work here. Unlike the hospital, we cater mostly to local people, not visitors and tourists. I've passed my language exams to practise here, but sometimes my accent leaves a bit to be desired.'

She grinned up at him, and Joe's heart inexplicably missed a beat. Bel reached into her handbag, pulling out a sheaf of paper and handed it to him. 'My curriculum vitae.'

Generally, if Joe could get a volunteer who'd already gone through the rigorous screening and interview process that the hospital put its employees through, he skipped the CV part of the process. But when he went to hand the papers back to her, Bel frowned at him. Maybe she was keen to prove that prosperous Chelsea hadn't played its part in getting her this far in her career.

'Thanks, I'll take a look at it later if I may. Perhaps I can show you around?'

She nodded. 'Yes, I'd like that.'

Bel took some time looking at the photographs of the clinic's volunteers in the reception area, and then they moved on to the first-floor consulting rooms and the cramped office that Joe shared with anyone who wanted somewhere quiet for paperwork. Then back downstairs again, to the semi-basement, where there were more consulting rooms, an art therapy room and a gym.

'This is the largest part of the clinic—the building's on a slope so at the back the basement becomes the ground floor…' He stopped to switch on the light at the top of the staircase and Bel hurried ahead of him, disappearing past the curve in the stairs, obviously eager to explore. The light flickered, and he heard Bel call out to him, a note of urgent command in her voice.

'Joe! Switch the light off!'

Automatically he flipped the light back off again, hurrying downstairs to find out what the matter was. Then he saw it…

She was standing on the last stair but one, looking down at a dark pool of water that extended along the corridor and seemed to be coming from the open door of the gym. Joe froze in horror. His brainchild. His passion…

'We need to switch the water off. And the electricity.' Bel's voice cut through the shock. She motioned towards a light fitting in the corridor, and he saw water dribbling from it.

He moved. Back upstairs to the utility cupboard, behind Reception. In a daze, he switched off the main electrical supply. The stopcock for the water supply refused to budge at first, but he gingerly applied his strength to it and it turned.

'Has it stopped?' he called down to Bel.

'I think so. Seems to be slowing a bit.'

Joe muttered a curse under his breath. Slowing a bit wasn't enough, the rooms downstairs must already be waterlogged. But there was no time to worry about the heavy weight of what felt almost like grief which had suddenly landed on his shoulders, robbing him of the ability to think straight. He needed to get back downstairs and see what he could salvage from the mess.

He grabbed a torch and made for the stairs. Bel wasn't anywhere in sight but her pumps and soft leather handbag, propped on the bottom step, gave him a clue. When he reached the basement corridor he saw her standing in the gym, her skin-tight jeans rolled up to her calves.

'This is where it's coming from.' She pointed to a dripping hole in the ceiling. 'It's slowed down a lot—it was pouring through before you switched the water off.'

Joe walked over to the hole, feeling his trainers begin to squelch as they absorbed water. He could feel Bel at his side, or rather smell her scent. Delicate and expensive, a stark contrast with the mess around them. He held out his arm, stopping her from going any closer to the mess of plaster on the floor.

'Stay there, I'll go and get a ladder.' He handed her the torch and hurried to fetch the stepladder from the large cupboard in the hall, returning to find Bel had ignored him and was standing right under the hole in the ceiling, shining the torch upwards. When he chivvied her out of the way, she retreated to the rehabilitation steps, sitting down and pulling her feet up out of the water, watching him solemnly.

He *had* to stop thinking about every little move she made, as if that were the most important thing he had to deal with at the moment. Joe climbed the stepladder, shining the torch into the cavity between the ceiling and the floor upstairs. The news wasn't good and it was surprisingly comforting to have someone here, to give it to.

'I can see where the water pipe's burst—it's at one of the joints and it's come apart completely. Some of the water's gone downwards but…' He shone the torch into the cavity, looking carefully at the ceiling joists. 'It looks as if it's travelled across as well, so it'll be dripping down into the other rooms.'

'We should go and look. May as well get that over with,' Bel mused as he climbed back down the ladder.

'Why don't you go home? I'll need to get a plumber in and start getting everything dried out—' The words dried on his lips as Bel got to her feet. Standing on the second, shallow rehab step, she was practically eye to eye with him, her hands on her hips.

'You're going to send the only volunteer in the place home, when you have an emergency to deal with?' She shook her head, as if he was a recalcitrant child. 'What sort of manager *are* you?'

There were a lot of answers to that, but only one that he could give at the moment. 'If you don't mind, staying to help out…'

Bel rolled her eyes, stepping down onto the floor. The top of her head barely reached his shoulder, but it still felt as if she was more than a match for him. 'I don't mind. It's far better than being moved out of the way when there are things to be getting on with.'

Bel could have been a little more tactful. But something about Joe, his delicious bulk and his obvious distress at seeing the damage… Bel had always had a soft spot for a gentle giant.

Joe could stay right where he was, though, in the nice-to-look-at-but-out-of-reach zone. Even if he did have blue eyes that seemed to change with the light, darkening to the colour of the ocean in the shadows of the gym. And even if she did reckon that spending a little more time outside might bleach his light brown hair to a delicious natural shade of blond. That was none of her business, nor were his strong shoulders and the hands which clearly knew exactly how to be tender. She'd made up her mind that she wasn't in the market for a new relationship, and what good were resolutions if you didn't stick to them when the going got tough?

Now was a time for practicality, though. You saw a need and you moved heaven and earth to meet it. And in less than three hours there would be patients knocking on the door. Presumably Joe would have enough volunteers to meet that need, but he didn't have anywhere for them all to go.

Then he smiled at her. Bel had summoned up the nerve to silently challenge him to send her home if he dared and it must have shown on her face, because he held his hands up in a gesture of surrender.

'Offer gratefully accepted. Since your Italian's

probably much better than mine, how do you feel about phoning round to find someone who can provide us with dehumidifiers? As cheaply as possible…'

Bel nodded. She could do that, but she wasn't leaving Joe alone down here to face the damage all by himself. That was just plain good manners. 'Okay, let's take a look around, and you can tell me exactly what you're going to need.'

Joe nodded, his jaw setting as if he were steeling himself for the worst. There was an art therapy room next to the gym, which almost broke Bel's heart, with ruined pictures peeling from the walls and other projects soaked and spoiled. He hurried her out of there into two consulting rooms, both of which had soaked carpets and water dripping out of the mattresses on the patient couches. The two smaller rooms at the back of the property were a little more encouraging. There were water stains on the ceilings and the carpets were wet in places, but nothing that wouldn't dry out and be put right easily. Joe opened the windows and a door at the end of the corridor which led out into a walled garden, letting a warm breeze into the chill of the basement.

'I reckon…just give them the size of the four rooms at the front, and let them tell us what they think we'll need. We can compare prices and make a decision.'

Bel nodded. She had a better idea but she'd tell him about that if and when it worked.

He could hear her voice drifting downstairs from the reception area as he mopped the tiled floor of the corridor, trying to make a start on getting as much water out of the place as he could. Bel's tone was warm and conversational but business-like, and Joe wondered whether he'd be able to deny her anything if she tried those tactics with him. Three-quarters of an hour later he heard her calling him, and walked back up the stairs.

'I've got three quotes.' She was sitting at the reception desk, her phone in front of her. 'You want the good news or the bad news?'

'Bad news first.'

She slid a sheet of paper towards him and he sat down. Just as well—the cost of this was eye-watering…

'Now for the good news.' She handed him a second sheet of paper, clearly unable to resist a slight flourish as she did so. Joe focused his eyes reluctantly onto the page. Even the best news he could imagine wasn't going to get the job done.

'This is…it's much better. Are they a reputable company?'

She tilted the screen of the receptionist's computer around and he saw a very professional-looking website. 'They're the best. Very well regarded—look at the reviews.' She clicked a link, displaying a string of five-star reviews. There *had* to be a catch, surely…

'How did you get such a good quote?'

'A successful company is more likely to be in a position to give a discount on a job that'll enhance its reputation. I went to the three best firms in the city and told them that we're a free clinic, doing important work.' She smiled at him. 'Then I begged a little.'

He doubted that. 'You begged?'

She shrugged. 'Maybe it was more a case of asking nicely. One of them wouldn't give me a discount, and two did. This is the best one, and they said they could send a plumber this morning to fix the pipe.'

'And what's the catch?'

'Don't be such a cynic. There's no catch. I just said that we'd give them a good review if they didn't cut any corners on the job. You can do that, can't you?'

Joe nodded. 'I'll give them the best review I've ever written if they do it for this price. Are you sure this includes everything?'

'Yes, positive. I spoke to the managing director at home…'

'Wait…' Joe held his hand up and she fell silent. 'You know the managing director?'

'No, but he's the one with the authority to do a good deed if he wants to. I spoke to someone at the office and told them that I was sure their boss would see this as an opportunity. Clearly, he did because he rang me back…'

Joe laid the paper down on the desk. Bel had done something that wouldn't have occurred to him, but she'd solved a problem and got the clinic what it needed for a really good price. 'Am I allowed to call him back and thank him? Tell him that I hope I'll be the first person he calls if there's anything I can help him with.'

She shot him a smug look. 'Too bad. I've already assured him that I should be the first person he calls—you can be the second, if you like. But you can speak to him to accept the quote if you like. *Lo sono molto grato...*' She snatched up the sheet of paper and called a number then slid her phone across the desk towards him.

'Yeah, okay, I think I can stretch to thanking someone.' Joe chuckled. He'd thought he was taking on a volunteer and found himself with a whirlwind on his hands. But right now, a whirlwind was exactly what he needed.

CHAPTER TWO

THE VOLUNTEERS WERE starting to arrive now, along with Maria, the receptionist. Joe had decided that the best course of action was to close the clinic for the weekend and offer video appointments which the volunteers could carry out from upstairs and, so far, his plan seemed to be working well. People were used to video appointments after going through lockdown and Maria had told Bel that no one had opted to reschedule so far.

Joe was busy co-ordinating the volunteers and speaking to patients and Bel set to work downstairs, speaking with the contractors when they arrived and doing what she could to clear the gym and the art room, along with the two consulting rooms that were the worst affected. It was hard work, and she had to call for help with the heavy gym equipment, but everyone was pulling together and doing what they could. If she'd been looking for testimonials to the clinic that Joe had created, then this was it. The clinic was obviously important to the people who gave their free time to work here.

He appeared in the doorway to the gym just before noon, and the look on his face said everything. Joe shook the hands of each of the workmen, thanking them, and then he turned to Bel. His smile replaced the weariness from backbreaking work, and she began to see only what had been achieved.

'This is...it's beyond great. Thank you so much.'

She felt a tingle of warmth travelling towards her fingertips. Bel had perfected the art of playing it cool, ever since Rory had broken her heart, and left her reputation in tatters, but Joe was a challenge that she hadn't anticipated.

'Looks a bit better, doesn't it? The plumber's almost done with the water pipe now, and the bits of plaster are almost all out of the carpet.' She gestured towards one of her own contributions to the cleaning-up process.

'It's marvellous. Can I ask one question?'

'Of course.' Bel looked around the room, wondering what had caught his eye.

'Where did you get wellington boots from, in Rome, in the summertime? And the socks to go with them?'

Bel looked down at her blue and white spotted boots. 'That's my secret. I got them when I went out for some LED lights, so that we'd be able to see what we're doing down here. You want a pair?'

He chuckled. 'Far too stylish for me—I couldn't carry them off. Are you thinking of going home any time soon?'

'No, I'm afraid you're stuck with me for the day. Why?'

'How do you feel about doing what you came here for? We've had a walk-in, someone who needs our help. She's summoned up the courage to come and I don't want to turn her away, so I was going to sit down with her and take her through exactly what she wants from us. Or you could, if you want.'

Bel could do with a sitting-down job right now, but she wasn't sure that she was up to this. 'I came here to learn. I don't have a lot of experience with the kind of work that you do here.'

'You can talk to people, can't you? Right now, all we want to do is find out what she wants from her rehabilitation, and what she thinks she's not getting elsewhere. And to reassure her that she's done the right thing in asking for help and that we'll do everything in our power to give her what she needs.'

'I'm…' Bel decided against telling him that she wasn't really dressed for the part. Neither was Joe, and he didn't seem to be worried about that. 'Okay. You'll be there?'

'I'll be there. I'm counting on you not needing me.'

'Everyone has a learning curve.' Bel tried not to sound too breathless about having Joe overseeing hers. 'I expect you to step in if I miss anything, or go beyond the clinic's remit.'

He nodded. 'Received and understood. How do you take your coffee? Maria's going over to the café across the street to get drinks for everyone.'

'I haven't had my morning cappuccino yet…' A takeaway coffee with milk after ten in the morning was generally considered to be something that only tourists asked for.

Joe pulled his phone from his pocket. 'I'll tell Maria. And tender your apologies.'

The woman sitting in Reception was hollow-eyed and her smile seemed to be more for show than an indication of how she really felt. Maria handed Bel a clipboard, which contained a form with the woman's details, gathered up a stack of paper cups from her desk and left them alone.

'Mrs Chiara Albertini?' Bel glanced at the form, holding out her hand to the woman. 'I'm Dr Trueman—Isabella.'

Chiara nodded, silently shaking her hand, and

Bel pulled one of the seats around to face her, sitting down. She recognised the way that Chiara seemed to have accepted defeat before they'd even started, because she'd started thinking that way herself with the long succession of lawyers who'd helped her fight Rory's claims about her…

Use the feeling. It's the only thing that makes it all worth it.

'This is hard, isn't it. I guess we're not the first people you've come to.'

Chiara twisted her mouth in an expression of regret, shaking her head.

'That's okay, it sometimes takes a while to find people who can give you exactly what you need. I'm new here as well, and I turned up this morning to find they have a flood in the basement, so today hasn't been going quite as planned…' Bel had lapsed into colloquial Italian now and she glanced at Joe, wondering whether he was keeping up. His brow was slightly furrowed but he said nothing, and Bel decided to take that as an invitation to continue.

'I did my homework before applying to join the team here, and I'm confident that this clinic will be the last place you need to come, even if it's not the first. But if I'm wrong, then here's my personal promise to you. You won't need to go through the process of looking again, because I'll do that for you.'

The beginnings of something ignited in Chiara's eyes. Surprise maybe, but it seemed that there was a little hope there, too. She smiled suddenly, making a subtle gesture, which asked Bel whether she wasn't overstepping the boundaries a little.

Maybe she was, but Bel didn't really care. Joe had put her in this seat, and she had a personal responsibility to her patients. She glanced at him again, and this time he responded.

'That's right. If we don't have the resources to help you, then we'll find someone who does. If we don't believe it's possible to help you, then we'll explain exactly why and give you the name of someone who can give you a second opinion, if you want one.'

Nicely put. Joe's expression had softened suddenly. Clearly, he wasn't quite as keen on throwing his patients in at the deep end as he appeared to be with his volunteers.

'Are we clear on that, then?' she asked Chiara.

'Yes. Would you like to see a copy of my medical notes?' Chiara reached into her handbag, taking out some sheets of paper, folded together. Bel glanced through them.

'Thanks. May I keep these for the file, please? I'd like to hear it in your own words as well, if you don't mind.'

Bel waited patiently as Chiara told her the

story. Her traffic accident, and the long stay in hospital. All of her other injuries had healed well, but after intensive therapy her dyspraxia was still a problem for her.

'I'm sure your doctors have already told you that dyspraxia takes different forms. Can you tell me a little more, and maybe some of the practical things that you can't do, which you'd like to?'

Chiara nodded. 'I have difficulties with judging distance and speed. Knowing where I am in relation to the things around me. I can be clumsy and disorganised…' She turned the corners of her mouth down.

'In my experience, people with dyspraxia are often quite well organised. They need to be,' Bel encouraged her gently and Chiara laughed.

'Yes, that's true. I manage well at home now. I keep everything very tidy and in the same place. And my therapist helped me to improve my co-ordination and motor skills.'

'And you're happy with that?'

'Yes. I'm still learning, but it's getting better.'

Bel nodded. 'That's great. So would I be right in saying that your hospital therapist has taught you things which will keep you safe and allow you to be independent? But there's something more now that you want to do?'

'Yes. It's an unimportant thing, really…' Chiara was nervous again now.

'If it's important to you, then it's important to me. Can you tell me about it, please?'

Chiara smiled. 'I used to sew.' She reached hesitantly into her bag, bringing out a wrapped package and cradling it protectively in her lap.

'Would you like to show me?' Bel asked and Chiara carefully removed the plastic and fabric wrappings and produced a piece of embroidery.

Bel caught her breath. 'That's beautiful.' There was colour and movement in the design that made it seem almost alive. 'You made this?'

'Before my injury. I was beginning to sell my pieces at craft fairs, but now I just can't do it any more. I have a little boy, he was born a few months before I had the accident, and I try to help him draw but…my drawing's worse than his. My husband draws with him but…' Chiara's eyes filled with tears.

Bel wanted so much to promise her that the clinic would help, but she honestly didn't know. She aimed her finest imploring look in Joe's direction, but his attention was on Chiara.

'You know that we can't guarantee success?'

Chiara nodded, turning her gaze onto him. 'I know. The thing I can't accept is not even trying.'

'We'll try. I have just the therapist in mind for you, Martina's very highly qualified, with a great deal of experience in helping people with dyspraxia. When her granddaughter was born she showed me some little dresses she'd made for her, so she understands the basics of sewing as well. How does that sound?'

A tear rolled down Chiara's cheek. 'That would be wonderful. Do you think she'd agree to see me?'

'I'm sure she will.' Joe got to his feet. 'Let me go and call her now, and we'll work out a time that suits you both—'

'Any time. I will come any time that she is able to see me. Tell her I would appreciate it so much, please, Dr Dixon. Thank you. And thank you, Dr Isabella.'

Joe grinned. 'We haven't done anything yet. I'm not going to be doing anything at all—it'll be you doing all of the hard work.'

'I'll work. Please, just give me a chance and I'll work hard.'

'Just do what you can, that's all we ask of you. You'll have the therapy that you want and a doctor will be assigned to you, to co-ordinate everything and answer any general health queries you might have. Since Dr Trueman has experience in treating head trauma and brain injuries, then—'

'Yes, of course,' Bel interrupted him. Maybe she shouldn't sound quite so pleased that Joe had obviously found the time to read the CV she'd given him. 'Perhaps we could think about any other things which are important to you and make a list, Chiara?'

Joe smiled at her, nodding in approbation. If a couple of reindeer decked out in jingling bells had just flown past the window it really couldn't have felt any more like Christmas. That wasn't an entirely professional attitude to take either, and Bel decided that it was time to stop trying to prove herself to Joe.

'I'll leave you to it and go and make that call.' He rose from his seat and Bel wondered if he felt two gazes fixed on his back as he left the reception area to go upstairs.

Then Chiara turned away, her eyes full of tears. 'Thank you so much, Dr Isabella.'

'It's my pleasure.' This wasn't the same as her work at the hospital, where success was measured in different and more immediately quantifiable terms, but it was just as rewarding. 'Now, let's make that list, shall we? And I'll also want to know about all the physical symptoms that you're still experiencing…'

The first floor was busy. Joe had rigged up makeshift cubicles so that the volunteers could video call their patients as privately as possible, and he decided that going downstairs would be his best bet if he wanted somewhere quiet to speak to Martina. The dehumidifiers were already set up and working and he walked out into the small walled garden at the back of the clinic to make his call, putting Martina on hold to phone up to Reception and check what time on Monday Chiara would be available for a video call.

Maria brought him his coffee, sniffing in disdain when he suggested that she might like to go home, since she'd already organised what everyone would be doing today and the clinic was officially closed. She was sure she'd find something to do, and he was to sit down for half an hour and take a break or he'd have her to answer to. Joe obligingly sank down onto the garden bench, feeling the muscles in his legs and back pull a little after a morning spent shifting furniture and computers.

This. It had taken a catastrophe for Joe to realise that this was what he'd worked so hard to create. People who refused to go home when he told them to. A separate identity for the clinic which allowed doctors and therapists time to concentrate on what came after hospital therapists had done their job. Chiara had reminded him how important it was to help people regain their sense of self.

The information pack that Joe had emailed to Bel explained all of that very carefully, and she'd clearly read it and put all of the principles it outlined into action. He hadn't needed to intervene and nudge the conversation back on track. She'd been perfect, right from the start. So much so that he was confident that Bel and Chiara would be managing just fine without him.

He closed his eyes, tipping his face towards the late morning sun. The shock of realising that the clinic would have to close for an unspecified period of time was wearing off now. Things were already on their way back to normal and the work was carrying on. He could dare to plan again, maybe even think about making a few improvements when the work of putting everything back together again was undertaken…

He was just considering a more practical flooring material for the gym, since the carpet was obviously ruined and would have to be taken up, when he heard the doors leading into the garden squeak open. Maybe they should do something about that as well… The thought was hastily parked at the back of his mind when he saw Bel.

She had a delicious air of animation about her. Somehow, her lips seemed redder and her dark hair more… Joe couldn't think of a word to describe it. More like the 'after' pictures in the ads for shampoo which demonstrated bounce and shine. Perhaps, in the unsettling experience of seeing the basement full of water, he just hadn't noticed that about her before.

'Happy?' The question seemed to be an important one to her.

'In what respect?' Joe decided not to mention that he was *very* happy to see her.

Bel rolled her eyes, coming to sit down next to him on the bench. 'With my performance.'

Something fell into place. Joe was driven over his work—he knew that. It had a lot to do with not being able to fully trust his relationships with people and turning to something he *could* trust. He'd fallen into the trap of defining Bel by her seemingly effortless grace, but maybe she felt that she had something to prove, too.

'I did look at your CV, even though it's probably not necessary since I've no doubt that the hospital put you through the same recruitment process as everyone else.' Something about that very obvious statement caused a flash of outrage.

'Of course they did.'

Joe resisted the temptation to ask why on earth they wouldn't. 'You've already done more on your first day than we could possibly have expected, if that's what you're wondering. Practically speaking, we'll be able to open again sooner because of the quote you got us. And medically speaking, you listened to Chiara and found out what she wanted, so that I could match her with a therapist straight away. What's not to like?'

That seemed to mollify Bel. 'So I've got the job?'

'It's not a job. You're volunteering.'

'And volunteers are second-best? Is that what this clinic is—a place for second-best people?'

Joe was beginning to like her forthright approach. He knew where he stood with her.

'No. Quite the reverse, in fact. I find that volunteers are often a lot more exacting than people who are being paid for what they do. Maybe passion is more persuasive than money for some people, and they're the people I want for this clinic. I can't expect to take all of their time, but a few hours is precious.'

Finally, she smiled. It seemed like an achievement of some sort, something he could luxuriate in for a moment.

'Right then. That's good.' Bel had been clutching the clipboard to her chest as if it might be needed as either armour or an offensive weapon, but now she proffered it to him as if it were a gift. 'I've made a list of the things that Chiara would like to work on. What happens next—I give this to Martina?'

Finally, an easy question. 'I'll show you how to enter it all on the computer system. Martina's recently retired and she'll be logging in from home before she speaks with Chiara on Monday.' Joe glanced at the closely written pages. 'Chiara's signed the data protection agreement?'

'Yes, Maria gave it to me when she brought the coffee. We read through it together.'

'Good. And Chiara understands what she can and can't expect from us?'

'Yes, I explained that every brain injury is different, and however hard we try we might not be able to help her regain all that she wants to. She knows that already, and reiterated what she said earlier. The thing she can't live with is not trying.'

Joe smiled, getting to his feet. 'We'll help her try. Actually, Martina will be forcing her to try when the time comes—it's not going to be an easy process. Since the office has been taken over for video conferencing, I'll go and get the laptop. This is as good a place as any to take you through entering everything onto the system.'

'I have mine here…' Bel produced a smart-looking device from her handbag, which appeared to have been carefully packed with anything that might be useful, and Joe smiled.

'Not yet. Before you connect your own devices to the system, we need to have *you* sign a data protection agreement and we'll have our IT guy check on your laptop's security. He's not available for a couple of weeks—he's a volunteer too, and he's on holiday at the moment.'

Bel nodded. 'Of course. Where do you get all of these volunteers from?'

Joe hadn't really thought about it. 'There's no particular strategy in place. I just know what we need and I ask.' Much as Bel had done this morning, only her approach had been a little more thought-out and she'd taken her request right to the top, which Joe very rarely did.

'It takes trust.' She was suddenly thoughtful. 'Expecting the best of people.'

It took audacity in Joe's experience, having the bad manners to ask busy people to give just a little more. Maybe trust on a different level from the emotional trust that Joe had long since decided wasn't for him. He decided that this wasn't a question he came equipped to answer.

'I'll go and get the laptop...'

CHAPTER THREE

BEL'S APARTMENT IN the centre of Rome was one of a dozen, arranged on two floors around a courtyard. It was quiet, and with a bit of careful planning it remained comfortably cool through the heat of the day and into the evening. But pacing up and down, questioning herself, was making her feel hot and bothered.

She flung herself down onto the sofa, wriggling out of her jeans. Pacing barefoot, the tails of her white shirt brushing the tops of her legs, was a great deal more comfortable but still not making her feel any cooler.

She'd messed up today, badly. Joe was the kind of man that you could like on sight, good at what he did and clearly happiest in his skin when he had a medical problem to deal with. Particularly gorgeous skin, she might add, which was heart-thumpingly consistent with the rest of him. She'd wanted him to like her back and she'd tried too hard to earn his approval.

He was right, she was a doctor with good experience and great references, and that should have been enough. But Rory had stripped away all of her confidence.

It had been a whirlwind romance. Rory had been working in the financial services department of her father's company and they'd met at a company day out. His attentiveness was flattering and when he'd asked her to marry him after only three months, telling Bel that when you knew, you knew, she'd been swept off her feet and accepted his proposal.

It had never occurred to her that he didn't see her at all, and that all he saw was her father's wealth. But even that wasn't enough for Rory. He'd spent her birthday weekend at her parents' house in Chelsea, and when they'd gone back to their own flat he'd seemed dissatisfied with their home, complaining that Michael Trueman's only child should be better supported by her father. She'd even forgiven that careless cruelty—Rory couldn't have known her parents had wanted a bigger family, but that her mother's pregnancy had been difficult and after Bel was born there had been no more children.

It was all so easy to see now, to count the red flags and the hallmarks of emotional abuse. But back then, she'd been blind to it all. She'd blamed herself for Rory's dissatisfaction and fought to keep his love, telling herself that she could be whatever he wanted her to be. He'd started to come home late, leaving her sitting alone waiting for him when they'd arranged to go somewhere together, and she'd made excuses for him.

Then, six months later, the scandal had hit. Rory was accused of making use of private information about her father's company to play the stock market, buying stock just days before a new venture was announced and the share price skyrocketed. It was just good luck, wasn't it? But the words 'insider trading' wouldn't go away, however much Bel believed in Rory's innocence. She'd hung on, refusing to believe her father's lawyers, until they'd presented her with the statement he'd written, implicating her in his money-making venture.

She *hadn't* taken her phone to her father's study, photographed the documents filed away in his desk drawer and then emailed them to Rory. Nor had she drawn up a plan for stock purchases and asked Rory to make them on her behalf, via several different shell companies that had been set up in her name. But it had taken a year to prove her innocence, and that year had taken its toll on Bel. She was no longer the confident young woman who knew she'd been lucky to have a privileged upbringing, but also knew that she'd achieved something on her own. She was someone who could, and probably would, be judged only as the daughter of a rich man. A person who had something to prove.

And now she was worried about what Joe thought of her. She'd tried to prove herself to him, even though he'd told her what she knew already—that her qualifications spoke for themselves. But still she'd put herself on trial, hoping he'd give her the reassurance of pronouncing her innocent. Had she learned nothing?

Pacing wasn't doing any good at all. Bel stopped by the coffee table, picking up her phone and staring at it, as if that might give her some answers. Surprisingly, it did. Her father had always been there when she'd wanted to talk.

He answered almost immediately. 'Hello, sweetheart. How's my favourite doctor?'

'Good. Finding my way around the hospital still.' Just hearing her father's voice made Bel feel a little better. 'What are you and Mum up to?'

'Your mother's gone to her book club cheese and wine evening, and so Wilf and I are fending for ourselves. He took me out for a run and now we're watching a film on TV, with a bowl of vegetable soup and some rather nice rosemary and garlic bread. All homemade and low in saturated fats, in case you were wondering…'

Her father had suffered a mild heart attack two years ago and that had been a wake-up call, for Bel and her mother at least, if not for him. He'd brushed off his doctor's advice, but Bel had made herself less easy to ignore and now her father had stopped working at weekends and had a much healthier diet. Wilf, the cocker spaniel, had more than enough energy to keep her father fit.

'No, Dad, I wasn't wondering. You're the one in charge of the changes you've made. Although I wouldn't mind knowing how your yearly check-up went.'

'Fine. My cholesterol and blood pressure are both down and Dr Humphries was very pleased with the twenty-four-hour ECG report. He congratulated me on obviously having followed his instructions to the letter.' Her father chuckled. 'I didn't let on about your intervention, he seemed so pleased with himself.'

'Good thought. Send me the ECG report, I'll take a look and let you know exactly what it all means.' Dr Humphries had done all of the right things, but her father didn't respond well to a list of dos and don'ts. He'd built his multi-million-pound business by thinking out of the box and making innovative decisions and Bel had approached him on that level, explaining everything to him and challenging him to take charge of his own health. That, her mother's cooking and the gift of a puppy had done the trick.

'Thanks, will do. How's your day been?'

Bel puffed out a breath. She'd been hoping that the conversation might take her mind off Joe.

'Interesting. I've volunteered to help at a free clinic which helps people in rehab. The next step in the process after we see them at the hospital.'

'You're thinking of expanding your scope of operations? How did that go?'

Dad had a habit of putting things in business terms, and an idea occurred to Bel.

'Actually... Would you mind if I asked your advice on how I might raise some cash?'

Her father chuckled. 'Ask away. That's my area of expertise...'

The beginning of the week in the trauma department of the hospital was busy, as the number of tourists in Italy's capital began to swell. Joe found himself working alongside Bel in A&E and at the outpatient clinic, and mutual respect for each other's skills, combined with having little time to think about anything but work, had allowed them to settle into a more companionable relationship. Bel still took his breath away and her smile never failed to make his heart beat a little faster, but Joe was dealing with it.

On Thursday they both happened to be travelling in the same direction for a minute or two and Bel gifted him with a scintillating smile. 'How are things going?'

'The basement's almost dried out now. It's looking much better than when you last saw it.' Joe decided not to mention the next stage, which was now occupying his thoughts during the evenings spent at the clinic. The insurance would take a while in coming through, and might not cover everything that needed to be done…

'Great. I don't suppose you're free for a coffee some time? It's to do with the clinic…' Someone beckoned to her urgently. 'Sorry. I'm busy with a patient at the moment, but perhaps I could catch you later to make a date?'

Bel hurried away, leaving Joe suddenly hungering for coffee. Since it *was* to do with the clinic and not a social invitation, he'd be justified in making himself free whenever Bel wanted to see him, but tonight was clearly out since Bel was busy and he was about to go off shift.

His phone bleeped, the familiar tone of the hospital's paging system telling him that he wasn't going anywhere just yet. He accepted the case, and made his way to the consulting room indicated on his screen.

Bel was already in attendance, along with an anaesthesiologist, and she left the young woman who was lying on the couch in his care for a moment, giving Joe a querying look.

'When I called for another doctor to assist, I

didn't realise they'd be paging you. Shouldn't you be leaving in a minute?'

'Nope. Are you leaving?'

She smiled up at him. 'Nope.'

'Fill me in, then.'

'Lydia Crawford, aged twenty-one, she's a tourist from America. She came off a motorbike and has a displaced ankle fracture and second degree road rash on her left arm. She was in a lot of pain and I called the anaesthesiologist to administer a sedative, since she'll have to go into surgery to have her ankle realigned.'

Joe nodded. The road rash, caused by dragging along stones or asphalt, would need to be cleaned and irrigated, which was a painful process. 'You've decided to deal with both her ankle and her arm at the same time?'

'If we can. It'll be easier on her, I think.'

'Yeah. Which do you want me to take?'

Bel seemed surprised at the idea. 'Won't you be taking the lead? You're the senior doctor.'

He supposed he was. Her CV had told him that he was five years older than she was, and that Bel had only recently completed her six years of specialty training. But he knew full well that it would have equipped her to lead a team in the operating theatre, and Joe had never been inclined to pull rank on younger doctors.

'We don't do that here.' Some did, but Joe

didn't. 'We're all doctors, and you know best how to deal with your own patients.'

Bel thought for a moment. 'Okay. I'd like you to concentrate on her leg, please. I'll deal with the road rash on her arm.'

Unusual choice. In Joe's experience, many doctors were all about the higher profile attached to surgical procedures, and would have left the painstaking process of tweezing debris from a patient's arm to whoever came to assist them.

'You're sure?'

Bel nodded. 'I had a tutor who had a particular interest in this kind of injury, and she taught me a lot. I think I can do well for Lydia.'

That put Joe in his place. If he'd been thinking that Bel was trying to please him, then he'd been mistaken. She'd already moved on now, turning to the nurse who was in attendance.

'Will you get Lydia ready for surgery now, please. Dr Dixon and I will go and speak to the boyfriend, and then scrub up.'

The nurse nodded, and Joe followed Bel out of the consulting room and into the waiting area. She consulted her phone, looking up and scanning the handful of people who were waiting for news of their loved ones.

'Luke Matthews?' Her gaze settled on a young man with sun-bleached hair and a badly scuffed leather jacket. It looked as if he'd come through the accident better than his girlfriend.

'Yes…' He held up his hand, getting to his feet and walking towards Bel. 'I'm waiting for news of Lydia Crawford.'

'Hi, I'm Dr Trueman. Will you come with me, please.' Bel took him to one side, motioning for him to sit down with her. 'Lydia's going to be okay, but I'm afraid she's broken her ankle, and will need a short surgical procedure to realign the bones. She also has some nasty scrapes on her arm, which need to be cleaned and dressed. But she's in good hands and she'll mend.'

Luke nodded. 'Can I see her?'

'Not right now. She was in pain and an anaesthesiologist has sedated her. They're getting her ready for surgery and perhaps you'd like to go and get a drink and something to eat—there's a nice cafeteria here in the hospital. Come back in an hour, and the receptionist will be able to tell you where Lydia is.'

Luke heaved a sigh. 'We've got train tickets for Paris tomorrow. I don't suppose…?'

Bel shook her head. 'We'll be keeping her here overnight and tomorrow at least—her leg's very swollen and we may need to make adjustments to her cast. And, of course, Lydia needs time to recuperate after her surgery.'

'How long will that take? I really wanted us

to see Paris together. I'm a Fine Arts major in college...' Luke took Bel's stunned silence as an invitation to elaborate on his theme. 'Lydia really likes that old film where they ride through Rome on a motorcycle, and we thought it would be fun. I *told* her that I should drive—none of this would have happened if she'd listened to me.'

'Luke...' Joe heard a trace of steel in Bel's tone. 'When she first came in, Lydia asked me to call her family, and I've passed their number over to our patient care team. We'll be liaising with them over what comes next, and my advice to them, and to Lydia herself, will be that she doesn't travel until she's well enough, which certainly won't be tomorrow. I dare say she'd appreciate a visit from you, but please concentrate on reassuring her rather than blaming her for spoiling your holiday. Do you understand me?'

'Yes. Okay...thanks, Doctor.' Luke turned the corners of his mouth down, shaking his head, and Bel rose from her seat. As soon as her back was turned, Luke grimaced up at Joe. 'Can you believe that?'

No, not really. Joe was surprised that Bel had let Luke off so lightly but, in all fairness, she didn't have time to give him a more thorough telling-off and it was beyond her remit to call him a selfish idiot.

'Listen to the doctor. Do as she says.' He turned

his back on Luke, and followed Bel towards the operating suite.

He caught up with her in the scrub room, where she was clearly taking her frustration out on her own fingers.

'Steady on. It's not worth scrubbing until you're red raw over. What's the film they were trying to recreate?'

Bel relaxed suddenly. 'Haven't you seen *Roman Holiday*? It's an old black and white classic.'

'I don't watch too many films. I'm not a big fan of happy endings. I generally find myself wondering when the other shoe's going to drop.'

'You'd love this one, then. It's very sad at the end.'

'They fall off the scooter?' Joe chuckled.

'No, they…' Bel stopped herself, pressing her lips together. 'I'm not going to tell you. That would spoil it for you if you ever *did* get around to watching it.'

He probably wouldn't. Unhappy endings didn't do much for him either. 'Well, the ending to this particular scooter ride is that I'll be going up to the ward when we're finished here, and letting them know that they're to keep an eye on Luke. He'll be out of there before he knows what's hit him if he doesn't behave himself. They'll be keeping Lydia's parents informed as well, and making sure she gets to speak with them as soon as she can—they're very used to dealing with cases where patients' families are abroad.'

Bel nodded. 'Thanks. That's great. I was expecting they would but it's nice to hear.' She took a paper towel from the dispenser and dried her hands. 'Let's put this young lady back together again, shall we?'

Joe was a dream to work with. Focused and yet always aware of where she was and never straying into her space. They worked side by side, Bel on Lydia's left arm and Joe on Lydia's left leg, communicating with each other by just single words.

Bel stood back to stretch her arms while Joe closed the incision on Lydia's leg. She watched as he expertly stitched the wound and scooted quickly out of the way as he stepped back.

He grinned suddenly. 'Out of my road, Doctor.'

Bel smiled back. 'You stay out of mine, Doctor.'

One moment of eye contact, which seemed to reverberate through her like a caress. Then they were both back to business.

'I'm finished with the ankle. You want me to irrigate?' Joe nodded towards the pieces of grit and debris that remained under Lydia's skin.

'Yes, thanks.' There wasn't too much more to be done now, but having Joe clean the wounds as she went would decrease the amount of time that Lydia needed to be kept under the anaesthetic.

They went back to work, closer now. When Bel judged that all of the debris had been removed she dressed the wound and Joe looked up at the clock.

'Forty minutes. Not bad going.' He glanced at the anaesthetist, who nodded back at him. The procedures had gone like clockwork and Lydia could start to recover now. 'I'll go up to the ward and speak with them, then get Reception to give Luke a call. Maybe remind him that Lydia's the one who needs care and attention right now, not him.'

'Thanks.' Bel smiled up at him. 'Are you going to the clinic when you leave here, or can I buy you that coffee? There's something I want to ask you.' She'd had her doubts when her father had suggested the solution to all of the clinic's problems, but it was too good an offer to turn down. She hoped that Joe would see it that way, too.

'I'm going to give the clinic a miss tonight. Maria called me earlier and there's nothing that I can do there right now. I didn't get any lunch, so was thinking of getting something to eat if you want to join me?'

Bel nodded. 'Yes, I only got to eat half my lunch before I was called away. Something to eat sounds like a good idea.'

Half an hour later, they walked out of the main entrance of the hospital. Bel was wearing a dress today. Retro in tone, with soft, folding skirts that foamed around her legs as she walked, and a fitted bodice. The bright red pattern was an invitation to look at her and her dark hair, swept up in an effortlessly perfect pleat at the back of her head, reminded anyone who cared to look that this was a woman who was more than capable of dealing with any attention that she got. She'd finished the look off with a small red handbag, looped over her arm. Joe's open-necked shirt and trousers felt a little pedestrian next to her style.

'You're going somewhere later on?' It was probably a little too early in their friendship to tell her that she looked nice, and if he plucked up the courage to do so, *nice* wouldn't have covered all he wanted to say. Bel looked fabulous.

'No.' She shot him a querying look and then glanced down at her dress. 'I got up this morning and thought that today could do with some colour.'

She'd succeeded in that. Even here, in Rome, Bel dressed traffic-stoppingly well. And it was clear that she dressed to please herself and not anyone else, which somehow pleased Joe more than he could say. The thought of walking her home in the warm softness of a darkening city sky reared its head and he decided that maybe they shouldn't spend too long over dinner, and part before that became a possibility.

'There's a nice place along here…' He indicated a side road and Bel nodded, following him to the small eatery.

She seemed a little nervous, suddenly. Fair enough, he was inexplicably as nervous as a kitten, and he reminded himself that this was just an impromptu meal for two colleagues who had things to discuss. He chose a table outside, under the shade of a large awning, and Bel deposited her handbag on the table and sat down.

'I have something to propose. An idea for the clinic…' She ignored the menu completely and when the waiter approached them Joe picked up the drinks menu instead and suggested a glass of wine. She nodded, pulling her handbag onto her lap and fiddling with the metal clasp.

'Go on, then. I'm listening.' He felt rather more at ease with listening to ideas and then trying to fashion them into some kind of plan than he did with Bel's dazzling smile.

She took a deep breath. 'It seems to me that the biggest challenge you face right now is keeping the clinic running while you wait for the insurance money to come through.'

Joe nodded. 'Yes. That and the fact that it may not be enough to pay for getting new things where they're needed. We set the place up on a shoestring and a lot of the gym equipment was second-hand, from a place that was closing down.'

'Then...perhaps I can help.' The waiter had brought their drinks and she reached for her glass, her hand trembling slightly as she took a sip of wine. Then she opened her handbag and took out an envelope, proffering it.

He only had a few moments to wonder at the oddness of it all, and then he opened the envelope and saw what was inside. The banker's draft, made out for a substantial amount of cash and originating from a London bank, made his jaw drop.

'What's this, Bel?' He resisted the temptation to ask all of the other questions that had flooded into his mind. How had Bel managed to raise all this in less than a week? Where had it come from? And what on earth was she doing, giving it to the clinic?

It appeared that she wasn't going to answer any of the unspoken queries. 'It's a donation. From a benefactor who'd like to remain anonymous.'

Joe stared again at the banker's draft, picking up his glass in an effort to buy some time to think. This would solve every last one of the clinic's current problems. But it wasn't a few euros added to the box that Maria kept under the reception desk, which might very well be accepted without knowing who the donor was.

'This is very generous. But with a sum like this I have a duty to manage the clinic's finances properly. That means knowing where this money came from.'

Bel twisted her mouth, clearly trying to work out what she did, and didn't, want to say. That wasn't making Joe feel any more confident about this. 'I didn't rob a bank or anything. It's all absolutely above board.'

'I'm not accusing you of anything. But I'm sorry, before I accept this I do need to know.'

She puffed out a breath. 'Dad told me you would. He said anyone worth their salt…' She closed her mouth, obviously feeling she'd said a little too much, and Joe consoled himself with the idea that *someone* thought he was doing the right thing. Maybe not entirely for the right reasons, he had to admit he was curious, but he'd keep that to himself until he knew a bit more.

'My father is Michael Trueman.' For a moment Joe couldn't place the name, other than that it made sense that he and Bel should share a surname. 'Michael Trueman of Trueman Industries. You've heard of them?' She tossed her head in a gesture that indicated he might not have done.

That was false modesty, and cold, hard anger started to swell in his chest. *Everyone* had heard of Trueman Industries and its founder, the man who'd built a multi-million-pound company from nothing but good ideas and hard work. The notion that he needed to re-evaluate everything about Bel made him suddenly feel a little sick. It was the same feeling that had accompanied his dealings with adults when he was a child, and the knowledge that they were likely to make inexplicable decisions about him which he had no control over.

'I've heard of them. You got this from the charity that the company runs?' It was well known that the charity supported organisations that were considered to be innovative in their approach, and Joe liked to think that the clinic was that.

Bel rolled her eyes. 'No, of course not. Charities take their time in making grants to organisations—there's a whole process that needs to be gone through. And anyway, it would look a lot like favouritism if they supported a place where I was volunteering, wouldn't it?'

True. At least Bel hadn't gone that far, but the alternative was just as unpalatable. 'So…what?

You called your father and asked him for the money?'

'No, I did not! Who do you think I am? I called my father to find out how he was doing because…well, because he's my father. And he needs to watch his cholesterol levels and I'm not having him sneaking cream cakes just because I'm out of the country. But I also asked him if he had any ideas about what I could do to help the clinic raise some money. Because, believe it or not, that's what he's really good at.'

Bel's cheeks were flushed with anger now, and she drained her glass, signalling to the waiter for another. He came immediately, maybe recognising what Joe had failed to understand. She was a rich girl who could do anything she liked, and she lived in a world that was way beyond his reach or understanding.

'I'm sorry.' The apology did little to mollify her, and Joe wasn't entirely sure he meant it. 'Your father agreed to donate the money. At your request.'

'No! That's not the way we do things, so you needn't start getting angry over that. I'm not some trust fund kid who calls Daddy every time she wants a new toy.'

And he'd thought that he was concealing his own view of this so well. 'What *did* happen, then? This is not idle curiosity, Bel. As director of the clinic I really do need to know.'

Bel took a gulp of her wine. Maybe he should order something to eat, but the waiter seemed to be ignoring him.

'We talked about it. Dad said that the real issue was cash flow—he was assuming you'd be sensible enough to have insurance…?' She raised an eyebrow in query.

'Yes, I like to think I'm sensible enough to have insurance as well.' That sounded combative, but maybe Joe meant it that way. No one was going to write him off just because he wasn't one of the powerful people in this world.

'Right then. So what you need is a bridging loan, and probably something to make up for what the insurance doesn't pay for. We talked about that a bit, and Dad said he liked what I'd said about the clinic, and that he wanted to make a donation. What was I going to say? *No, sorry. It's the answer to all of the clinic's problems, but your money's not good with them.* I doubt he'd take that particularly well—who would?'

'I know this is a kind gesture, Bel, and I appreciate it. But your father doesn't know anything about the clinic. How can he give this much money and know it'll be well used?'

Bel looked as if she was about to explode. 'He

took my word for it. He's my father, and he trusts me. Unlike you, obviously.'

Joe picked up his glass, and then put it down again, deciding that wine was only going to escalate things. Then he saw the tear in the corner of Bel's eye. This meant something to her—he wasn't sure what, but she wasn't just angry with him because she wasn't getting her way.

'Can we start this conversation again?'

She calmed suddenly, dabbing at her eye with a napkin. 'Yes. Let's start again. Only let's not talk about the money this time.'

Joe could see her point. The money really wasn't the problem here, which was a lot to say for an amount this generous. *They* were the problem, and that was a much more difficult proposition.

He was attracted to Bel. He could admit that to himself, if not to her. And the very same vulnerabilities, the reasons he couldn't trust anyone in a relationship, were the ones that had made him react so badly to her offer of money.

That might be okay if the money had been for him, but it wasn't, it was for the clinic. He had no right to reject it because of his own hang-ups. And somewhere deep inside he knew that he'd treated Bel unfairly, and that he owed her an explanation.

'Yeah. You're right. Shall we have something to eat?'

She nodded, gesturing to the waiter, who seemed to have magically reappeared from somewhere, and ordered a snacking plate for two. Then she turned her bright, clear gaze onto him. 'Seems we both have some explaining to do.'

CHAPTER FOUR

BEL HAD WONDERED how Joe might react to her father's donation, and he'd very successfully managed to push all of her buttons. It wasn't much consolation that she'd clearly managed to push a few of his in return.

But walking away and never speaking to him again wasn't an option. There were the practical considerations—they worked together and how else was the clinic going to get the money at such short notice? And Joe's commitment and the way that he cared about people were values that Bel cared about, too.

He'd clearly readjusted his view of her, though, and that hurt. Maybe people had always thought of her differently because of who her father was, and Bel just hadn't noticed it before.

They'd picked at the snacking plate in silence, which had given Bel the chance to calm down and assess the situation. She and Joe needed to find a way to agree about her father's donation, for the clinic's sake. That was what mattered. Her pride came second to that.

'Don't… Just listen to what I have to say, please.'

'Say whatever you want. I'll listen.'

Bel took a breath. 'I know exactly how lucky I am. My parents were in the position to give me everything, and they had the good sense not to. Mum and Dad have a really nice house, in a lovely part of the world, but…they could live anywhere they wanted and it's not ostentatious. I had every opportunity they could give me. I went to a good school and we travelled as a family during the school holidays, even if Dad usually worked a bit while we were away. But it was always up to me to take advantage of those opportunities. When I went to medical school Dad gave me the cash to buy a reliable second-hand car and I had to go out and find something to get me from one place to another.'

Joe nodded, smiling. The kind of smile that would have been the same whatever she'd said.

'I didn't talk too much about my family, but it was no secret. No one can buy their way through medical school, and I had to work just as hard as everyone else. You know that.'

Maybe she was trying a little too hard to gain his acceptance, but it seemed that Joe's face had softened a little. He opened his mouth to say something and then closed it again, obviously remembering his promise to say nothing. But Bel wanted to hear his reaction.

'Go on. Say it.'

He shrugged. 'Just that…your childhood is a very long way away from my experience. But you should never have to feel ashamed of it, or that what you've achieved on your own is any the less for it.'

'Thank you.' The words slipped out before Bel could stop them.

'Who made you feel like that?' Joe's gaze seemed to slide past all of her defences.

'There was someone… I was serious about him. When he left me, it became very obvious that he'd only been with me because of who my father was and… He was involved in some fraudulent dealings on the stock market, and when he was caught he said that it was all my idea and I'd actually been the one to steal the insider information he used. He had some so-called proof. He'd used my phone to photograph documents from my dad's desk and then emailed them to himself. There was an enquiry and I had to clear my name. That's why Dad made a personal donation. The trustees of his charity would have held an emergency meeting if he'd asked them, and assessed the clinic's application for funds as a matter of urgency. But he didn't want any suggestion of favouritism or financial irregularity, because he knew how badly that had already affected me.'

'I'm sorry.'

Those two words meant everything. Joe hadn't asked whether she actually *had* been innocent of the insider trading that she'd been accused of. He didn't question anything—he just believed her. Bel had learned just how much of a luxury that was.

'My dad knows how important rehab is—he had a heart attack two years ago. He had all the best medical care, but when he left the hospital he was very lost. His doctor was just telling him to do things without explaining properly. I was a doctor, so I could tell him the thinking behind everything, and let him take a few executive decisions of his own. Mum and I clubbed together and bought him a puppy for Christmas, and he and Wilf adore each other...' She saw Joe grin suddenly. 'What?'

'Sorry. I can't help thinking it's a little incongruous for Michael Trueman's wife and daughter to have to club together to buy a puppy.'

'No, it isn't! I mean... Mum could pay for a whole platoon of puppies just by wearing the same dress for Christmas that she did last year, but her wardrobe is the one thing that they don't apply the *not ostentatious* policy to. We're lucky enough that money isn't really the point, though. Wilf's a member of *our* family and we wanted to get him for Dad together. And he likes going for walks, which was the main point of it all.'

Joe had left the banker's draft on the table between them, seeming unwilling even to touch it, and Bel had stowed it back into her bag before it blew away in the evening breeze. She took it out, determined to offer it a little better this time.

'My dad personally understands the value of a clinic that helps people with the after-effects of illness or injury, and he trusts me when I tell him that the clinic is a project that deserves his support. There's nothing underhand about it, and I didn't persuade him against his better judgement. We'd both be grateful if you would accept his support for the important work you're doing.'

Joe stared at her. 'I… It's a very generous offer, and made with a graciousness that I don't deserve.'

She'd done her best, but Bel wasn't going to sit here all evening holding a money order while there was food and a remarkably nice glass of wine on the table. 'Go on, then. Deserve it.'

He chuckled. 'You're not going to let me off the hook, are you?'

'You want me to?'

'No, not really. After what you've said, there's

a part of me that has to explain why I reacted the way I did.'

And another part of him that didn't want to? Bel ignored the implication because she wanted to hear what was on Joe's mind. She put the banker's draft out of sight, under the heavy snacking plate.

'My childhood was different from yours, although we probably didn't grow up too far away from each other. My adoptive parents lived in a small house on the outskirts of Chelsea and they had to economise to make ends meet. But they had this fierce, uncompromising love that turned my life around.'

'How old were you when you were adopted?'

'Ten. My mother put me into local authority care soon after I was born, but she always refused to give me up for adoption, so I was fostered. As soon as I was old enough to misbehave, I managed to find a few creative ways of making trouble.'

'Wasn't that just a reaction to the situation?'

'Yes, I dare say it was. I didn't want to entertain the thought, but in retrospect I imagine I was pretty transparent. In all fairness, the adults had their hands tied as well because my biological mother wouldn't sign the adoption papers, and she spent a lot of time fighting to prevent me from being adopted.'

Bel nodded. If it was hard to listen to this, how hard must it be to say it? But Joe betrayed no emotion, just a kind of blank acceptance.

'But your adoptive parents got through to you.' If Joe had met their attempts to reach him with the same lack of emotion then that mustn't have been easy.

'Mum made it quite clear to me from the get-go that however clever I thought I was, however tough, she was ten times cleverer and twenty times tougher. And that nothing I could do would make her give me up. It took a while to get that through my head, but I finally realised that she really meant it. I settled down, stopped playing truant from school and… They were proud when I got into medical school. I used to tell them that they were right to be, it was largely their doing.'

'Your parents sound like really good people. Where are they now?' Bel hadn't missed Joe's use of the past tense when he'd referred to them.

'They were in their fifties when they took me on. They died four years ago.'

'I'm so sorry. You lost them both, together?'

'Within three months. Dad had been fighting cancer and I knew that his consultant didn't expect him to live for much longer. But Mum went first, from sudden cardiac arrest. After the funeral Dad told me he'd had a good life but he was ready to go now. I was with him when he died, and he seemed…peaceful.'

'It must have been very hard for you, though.'

Even that didn't seem to reach him, although he must feel something. 'They were the only people I've ever been able to trust. No one else was around for all that long.'

Bel thought for a moment. There was nothing more she could say, and Joe was shutting down, retreating from the realities of a goodbye that must have torn him apart. Maybe it was better to move on now, since that was what Joe clearly wanted to do.

'So allowing yourself to depend on my father's donation when you've never even met him would be a definite no-no.' She hardly knew Joe as well, but Bel didn't want to say that.

'It would be horribly ungrateful, in the face of an extremely generous offer of help.' Joe pursed his lips, obviously trying to negotiate his way between what he knew and how he felt. 'Don't think for a moment that I don't know I'm being unreasonable.'

'I didn't exactly help things along, did I? What are you expected to think when someone offers you a large amount of money with no explanation about where it came from?'

He shrugged. 'Don't make excuses for me, Bel.'

She couldn't get through to him. He was perceptive and very frank, but it was as if he were talking about a maths problem. He'd survived by keeping his emotions under wraps.

'We're very different, Joe. But I hope you can understand that I want some of the same things you do. The clinic's important.' More important to Joe than she'd thought. He clearly didn't have any family ties, and he'd poured all of his passion into the place. It was the one thing that he trusted enough to care about.

He nodded, sliding the envelope out from underneath the sharing plate. 'Is it too late to accept this?'

'No. What are your conditions? I can't imagine that you don't have some.'

'I'd like to account to your father for every penny we spend.'

'He didn't ask for that, and if he'd wanted it he would have. But I think he'd really appreciate the gesture. He told me that I shouldn't get involved with the financial side of things because…' Because of Rory. He had no place at this table. 'Maybe Dad's being a little over-protective.'

'This has to be between him and me, Bel. There's no reason why you should be involved, and I'd really rather you weren't after what's happened to you.'

Bel felt a little thrill of warmth radiate from

her heart. 'I'd like to take some before and after photos for Dad, though.'

Joe nodded. 'Sounds good to me. I'll make sure to take some too, during the week. Done?'

He held out his hand and Bel put hers into his. His touch was tender and this felt more like a lover's tryst than a handshake. 'Done. Anything else?'

He grinned suddenly. 'I get to buy an uptown girl dinner?'

Bel straightened in mock outrage. 'You can buy me dinner. Never, ever, call me an uptown girl again.'

Joe usually worked four days a week at the hospital so that he could spend all day on Friday at the clinic. He'd been busy, seeing patients and organising the clean-up in the basement, and had sat down for an hour to compose a thank-you note to Michael Trueman, enclosing a list that Maria had drawn up of the expenses so far. He'd just read it through for the second time when he saw Bel in the doorway of the office. She had tears in her eyes.

'What's the matter?' He jumped to his feet, wondering guiltily if this was a reaction to anything he'd done.

'Nothing…nothing…' She fanned her face with her hand. 'Happy tears. I just went down to the basement and put my head around the door of one of the consulting rooms.'

Ah. So she'd seen Paolo and Leonardo, both wheelchair users, along with several members of their families and friends. 'They all turned up this morning. They'd decided that now those rooms are dried out they could do a bit of painting. I told them that we didn't expect them to help, but they'd brought enough food to keep them going for about a week and were in no mood to take no for an answer.'

Bel plumped herself down on a stack of boxes and blew her nose. Today she was wearing a filmy leopard-print skirt, with a wide leather belt and gladiator sandals. She looked like a million dollars, but telling her that might prompt an indignant list of how cost effectively she'd put her outfit together. Joe contented himself with just thinking it, and watched as she flipped through photographs on her phone.

'I took some pictures. They're making a really good job of it.'

'Leonardo was a painter before he was injured, falling off a ladder. He promised me he'd keep everyone in order and make sure all of the edges were nice and straight, so I left them to it.'

Bel nodded. 'This one's a good one. Do you want me to send it to you, so you can send it to my dad?' She held out her phone and Joe took it. When he zoomed in on the line between the wall and the ceiling it was reassuringly straight, which meant that he wasn't going to have to explain to the volunteers using the room why they were going to have to put up with a less than professional job.

'I've just finished writing him a note, now.' Joe decided he didn't need to read the email through again, and pressed *send*. 'You send him whichever photographs you think he'll like. We'll keep the business side separate, shall we?'

She nodded, smiling. 'Yes. Thanks.'

The moment was broken by the sound of the clinic's alarm system. Bel jumped, looking around her.

'Basement.' Joe got to his feet, hurrying towards the stairs.

'How do you know?' Bel was right behind him, and it was no surprise that she had questions. Blindly following wasn't her style.

'The alarm console's in Reception. But since no one else is in the building, then I'm taking a guess…' He hurried down the stairs and reached the consulting room only moments before Bel caught up with him.

Paolo was lying on the floor, and Leonardo had already got the other helpers to stand back. He didn't look best pleased when Paolo tried to reach for his upturned wheelchair, telling him to stay put until help arrived.

'Thanks, Leo.' When everyone saw Joe in the doorway, the situation started to defuse a little. 'That's great, everyone—you all did the right thing.'

'All but one of us.' Leonardo was obviously annoyed about something, but Joe reckoned that would keep.

He didn't need to say a word to Bel. She'd already righted the wheelchair and was kneeling down on the other side of Paolo, waiting for Joe to go through the questions and examination that would tell them whether Paolo was unhurt or not.

'Okay. Looks as if you haven't done any damage, but don't brave it out if there's anything that worries you later on.' Joe lowered his voice. 'The next time you want to push yourself, make sure you do it when Max is here.'

Paolo nodded, his face twisted with disappointment. 'There was a bit that someone had missed and I reckoned if I stood I could reach it. I *can* stand, I do it with Max.'

'I know. Max is your therapist and he knows exactly how to do things safely with you. I have to trust you to listen to him. You want to stand for your wedding, and we're doing our best to get you there. You're just working against us by trying things you're not ready for yet, however tempting it is.'

'Sorry, Doctor.' Paolo had already been told not to try things on his own just yet, and he knew why that was. Joe knew it was frustrating, but he had to emphasise Max's advice.

'No harm done. Just think the next time, eh?' He beckoned to Leonardo's wife, who came over to steady the wheelchair, as she'd been shown during her sessions with her husband. Then Bel took up her position, and on his count they lifted Paolo back into the wheelchair.

'Thank you, Isabella. Dr Dixon.' Paolo reached to clasp Joe's hand.

'No problem. I'd go and have a word with Leo if I were you. He doesn't look too happy.'

Paolo nodded, moving over to Leonardo, who threw up his hands in a gesture of exasperation. The two men started to talk, and Leo reached for his friend, resting his hand on his shoulder. He'd taken on a role as unofficial mentor to Paolo, and it was time for Joe to go.

'That's harsh.' Bel had followed him silently, but delivered her assessment of the situation when they re-entered the office.

'Yeah. I know. Paolo has to stay within what he can do safely though…' Joe shot her a questioning look as she shook her head.

'I meant for you. That you have to be the guy who pulls him up on it.'

Joe shrugged. 'Paolo knows I want him to succeed. Leo understands his frustration, and it was time for me to step back and let him reassure Paolo. We can't always be the nice guys. We encourage our people to help and support each other and I feel that's one of our greatest strengths.'

She nodded. 'So we're the ones who get to read the riot act from time to time, then.'

'Yeah. You can do that, can't you?' There was no question in his mind that Bel could, and that she would if necessary.

'I can do it. Leo and Paolo each seem to have very different goals.'

Joe smiled. Sometimes it took volunteers a little while to notice that, but Bel had immediately seen the people and not the wheelchairs. 'Yeah. Paolo's not going to be able to walk for more than a couple of steps without his wheelchair, and he knows that. But, like a lot of wheelchair users, he can stand a little, and he really wants to make the most of that for his wedding in six months' time. Leo's getting involved with wheelchair sports now so his ambitions are different. He has an entry level sports wheelchair and he's looking to develop his fitness and find out what's right for him. The process isn't the same as in the trauma department of the hospital, where we have one, very well-defined, aim.'

'To do what's medically necessary.' Bel was obviously thinking this through.

'For the most part, yes. You didn't ask Lydia whether she thought that pieces of grit and tarmac in her arm were a good look or not—you knew you had to remove them to prevent infection and help the arm to heal. I dare say she understood that too. Later on, if she has any scarring, then what medical science can do will be all about how she feels and what she wants.'

Bel straightened a little, and Joe recognised the signs. She was about to take issue with him. 'Are you telling me that you think I botched the job, and that I'll leave her with scars?'

'No. It was just a *for instance*. What I meant was that rehab is partly about being able to do the things you have to do, but also about living your best life.' He liked the way that Bel always called his hand on things. Maybe he did play his emotional cards a little too close to his chest at times.

She was still thinking, and Joe could feel another question coming. 'Do you suppose…' She softened it with a smile. 'Are *we* living our best lives?'

Clearly, she'd been thinking about their conversation last night. And he already knew how direct Bel could be. 'I don't know about you, that's for you to decide. I'm not entirely sure about me either, but I feel passionate about the work we do here and at the hospital, and it gives me a lot of satisfaction. I think that's my best life.'

Maybe one element of a best life. Maybe Bel was another part of that life that had always seemed completely beyond him. Joe had always told himself that having one thing that he really wanted was enough.

She was silent, and he wanted to know what she was thinking. 'What do you reckon?'

'I think you're probably right.' Bel seemed as unenthusiastic about the idea as he felt at the moment. Perhaps it was time to move on.

'How's Lydia? Did you see her today?'

'She's...physically doing very well. Luke decided to take the train to Paris this evening, and she was a bit upset about that. She said that it was better to find out what his priorities were sooner rather than later, and I told her I could agree with her wholeheartedly on that score.'

Joe grimaced. Bel hadn't said how close her relationship with the man who'd betrayed her was, but she'd obviously been hurt very badly. 'So she's on her own here?'

'Her mother's going to fly out, and she'll be arriving on Sunday. That's what I popped in to ask you. We were going to go through some cases on Saturday, ready for me to start work with the clinic next week, and I wondered if we could put that off until Sunday. I'd like to go in and see Lydia, and cheer her up a bit if I can. It's no fun being in hospital in a strange city, with no one to visit.'

'Yes, of course. Sunday's better for me too. I need to spend some time on sorting out what we can do for ourselves and what we need to get contractors in for, and that's a lot easier when suppliers and contractors are in the office.'

'Thanks.' Bel smiled at him, her eyes flashing with mischief. 'Are you finished here? I could be persuaded to buy a guy dinner. On the understanding that neither of us has to share any more confessions tonight.'

That was Bel all over. She'd obviously worked out that Joe would be feeling awkward about that, and he guessed she probably did too. So she'd come right out and said it, to defuse the situation.

'I'll leave the thing about being a cat burglar for another time, then?'

She chuckled. 'Yes, please do.'

Maybe he *would* take a chance and spend an evening working on his definition of a best life. 'I'm done here. I think it's about time our volunteer painters went home, and dinner sounds good.'

CHAPTER FIVE

BEL HAD SPENT several summers with her parents in Rome, but this felt like the first time she'd really seen the city. Vibrant, new and different every day. At home with the past, able to keep the beautiful things it wanted and let go of those it didn't.

When she'd asked Joe whether he'd seen many of the treasures of Rome, it didn't come as much of a surprise to find that he hadn't. He'd been immersed in his work, and they'd had to wait. He'd told Bel that there was no fun in seeing the sights alone, and she'd taken that as a challenge.

Starting slow, she'd managed to persuade him away from the clinic on time for three Friday evenings in a row. The long queues at the Colosseum meant that exploring the inside was an all-day venture but seeing it from the outside was still an experience in feeling very small in the presence of its imposing bulk.

And then he'd texted her. This was a new development in their relationship—something that had nothing to do with the clinic or the hospital and wasn't a spur-of-the-moment decision. Joe was going to be working late at the clinic on Friday evening, but he was thinking of going to the art gallery in the Palazzo Barberini on Saturday afternoon, and wondered whether she would like to come along.

Bel's immediate reaction was that she wanted to go, but she hesitated. The wording of his text was casual enough, and it was a natural consequence of evenings spent together on an impromptu basis. But this was a plan, and one that involved meeting up for no other reason than the pleasure of each other's company. She was more drawn to the idea of seeing Joe than she was to staring at paintings, and that made it feel even more like a date.

'Don't be ridiculous,' Bel muttered reproachfully to herself. 'It's whatever you decide it is…'

That was enough of an excuse to text back and say she hadn't been to the Galleria Nazionale di Arte Antica in a long time and she'd like to revisit it. Joe spoiled the casual tone of the exchange slightly by texting back almost immediately, saying he'd be leaving the clinic at three, and maybe they could meet at the gallery at half past. Bel put her phone back into her pocket. She could maintain her distance by replying later.

Or she could reply now. She ignored the flutter of apprehension, the tiny voice in the back of her mind which questioned whether it was wise to get this close to Joe, and took her phone from her pocket again, texting him back to tell him that she'd arranged an appointment with Chiara for after lunch at the clinic, so she'd see him there.

It was always a thrill to see Joe after they'd been working apart for a couple of days, and when Bel saw Chiara out he was already waiting for her in Reception. Smiling and relaxed. Gorgeous. The gorgeous part of the equation was awkward, but Joe couldn't help it, and Bel could never stop herself from noticing it.

'Call me if there's anything.' He turned to Maria, who shot him an annoyed look.

'What is there going to be? We have plenty of other people here, we don't need you.'

'No, of course not. But call me if there is…' Joe hurried Bel out of the door before Maria could answer.

There was a reassuring distance between them as they walked along the busy streets towards the Palazzo Barberini.

'You like art?' Bel asked.

He nodded. 'I like people-watching and looking at faces. An art gallery is about the one place you're *allowed* to stop and stare. I used to love the National Portrait Gallery when I was a kid.'

'You went there a lot?' Bel had been to her share of art galleries when she was little, but it generally wasn't her family's first port of call when they went to a new place.

Joe shrugged. 'I'd been there on a school trip and something about the pictures fascinated me. Mum found out that I'd played truant to go back and see them again, and told me we'd make a deal. I went to school during the week and she'd take me to whatever museum or gallery I chose at the weekend. I insisted on looking around on my own so she'd find a bench and pretend to read, although I expect she was keeping a close eye on me.'

It was the first time since their argument over her father's donation that Joe had said one word about his childhood. The thought of a lonely blue-eyed boy, staring up at faces in paintings, tugged at her heart. She should probably let this go, but she couldn't.

'So you haven't entirely given up on London, then?'

Joe shrugged. 'One art gallery isn't really enough to make you want to live in a city. I started to look for jobs overseas after I lost Mum and Dad. London had far too many memories for me, and with them gone none of them felt like good ones. And I do like the sunshine and warm weather.' He gestured towards a rack of brightly coloured scarves outside a shop. 'They look nice. You want to have a look?'

'Give me a bit of credit, Joe. If that's all you want to say about it, that's fine. Don't try to divert my attention with scarves, because it won't work.'

He chuckled. 'Okay. Sorry. London's been well and truly left behind now and we're in Rome. And that's all I want to say. You really *don't* want to look at scarves?'

'No, I don't. Not those, anyway. As you so rightly say, you're in Rome now, and it's time to up your game if you're going to use clothes as a distraction.'

Joe clasped his hand to his chest as if mortally wounded, but he was smiling. Even their bickering seemed to bring them closer, heading unerringly towards territory that was dangerous for both of them. But Joe was showing no inclination towards turning back, and Bel didn't want to either.

Joe always paid his way, but Bel knew he couldn't afford to pay for her as well and they'd fallen into the habit of going halves on everything, even pavement coffees. When he'd bought his entry ticket he handed it over to Bel and she stowed it away in her handbag, along with hers.

As they walked towards the first gallery, she slipped her hand into the crook of his arm, in a silent message that he wouldn't be looking at *these* faces alone. Maybe Joe got that, and maybe not, but he smiled, laying his hand over hers in a signal that this was where she belonged. It was more than just companionship or solace. Bel was becoming used to the ever-present hunger to be closer to Joe and somehow it felt that this *was* where she belonged.

Art took on a new meaning. Bel had never thought of the faces in paintings as timeless, but today they were. Joe stopped in front of a portrait of an unknown woman, regarding it thoughtfully.

'What do you suppose she's thinking?'

Bel stopped to consider the question carefully. 'I'm not quite sure. Maybe she's decided not to give us any clues.' Bel had seen that expression before, in shops and in the street. In hospitals.

Joe nodded, turning the corners of his mouth down. 'Yeah. They're always the most challenging patients, eh?'

The most challenging people. That was one of the things that Bel liked about Joe—he was honest. He didn't just tell her the truth, he went further than that and told her what was on his mind and she had a very good reason to value that. It occurred to her that Joe did too, for different reasons.

'Let's move on, then.' She tugged at his arm and he smiled, walking with her to the next painting. 'Now, I know exactly what's on *her* mind.'

Joe stared at the painting. He seemed to see nothing of the ornate red dress or the carefully arranged fabric that covered the woman's hair, just the stray lock that fell across her forehead and the look in her eyes. 'Yeah, I think I do too. You first…'

The Palazzo Barberini wasn't just an exhibition space, the whole building was a masterpiece in itself, a baroque palace that was filled with frescoes and soaring pillared walkways. Eager to see everything, but knowing that would take far longer than just a few hours, they pressed on to see the throne room. The huge, empty expanse invited visitors to look up at the painted ceiling and lying on the floor to appreciate it was de rigueur here.

Bel picked her spot and lay down, wondering if Joe would follow. Of course he did. There was no mistaking the intimacy that had grown between them, suffusing every part of the afternoon with delight. Their feet were over a metre apart but their shoulders were pressed together as they stared up at the ceiling.

'I could stay here for ever.' Somehow his hand had found hers, his light touch allowing the gesture to be interpreted whichever way Bel wanted to. Right now, she wanted to interpret it as a promise for a future which was uncertain but would be all the better for having Joe in it.

'Me too. Maybe not *quite* for ever. We'd need cushions for that.'

'Yeah. A long time, though. Or until closing time, whichever comes first.'

'Closing time won't be long enough.' She tapped her forefinger against his, to emphasise the point. If Joe thought that they'd leave this behind when they walked out of the building then Bel hoped that he was wrong.

'You're right. Closing time definitely won't be long enough…'

Joe couldn't claim innocence over what was happening here. He'd known exactly what he was doing when he'd invited Bel to the Palazzo Barberini, and he'd gone ahead and done it anyway. All of his fears, his inability to trust that any relationship would last, meant that asking Bel on a date was out of the question. But he'd deliberately put himself in the romantic equivalent of harm's way—and when intimacy had unsurprisingly come to find him, he'd stood his ground.

They hadn't spent long enough looking at the ceiling in the throne room, but Joe wasn't sure that he could ever spend too long looking at a ceiling with Bel. He'd scrambled to his feet, pleased to find that she'd been slower than he was and given him the opportunity to help her up, and they moved on. This time he risked holding out his arm for her to take, and when she did, shivers ran down his spine.

They'd continued on their aimless trajectory, wandering through rooms full of art, where they could enjoy the wonderful silences between them as they stared at faces. One day, maybe soon, he could stare into Bel's eyes and see what she was thinking. The idea didn't fill him with as much terror as it should.

They hadn't been here long enough when seven o'clock approached and the palace started to empty out. He and Bel were amongst those who seemed determined to stay until the very last moment.

'Where shall we stop last?' Joe asked. Which moment would they take with them, out into the streets of Rome?

'The Borromini staircase,' Bel replied immediately, obviously having thought about this and chosen carefully from the treasures on offer here.

'Good thought. That's…' Joe looked around, trying to get his bearings.

'This way.' Bel pulled at his arm, leading him towards the elliptical staircase in the south wing of the building, which would take them back down to the main entrance.

Leaning over the stone balustrade, and looking downwards at the ever smaller oval repeats, clearly made Bel a little light-headed. She moved back suddenly, and Joe laughed. 'Maybe we'll do that when we get to the bottom, and there's nowhere to fall.'

'Yes. I've seen photographs and if we stand in the right place and look upwards it looks like a snail's shell. Seeing it first hand will be better, though…'

Joe nodded. Somehow they both understood that their time here couldn't be captured in just two dimensions. It was a matter of the heart.

Bel started to walk down the staircase and he hung back, waiting for her to complete a half turn before he set foot on the steps. She turned, obviously wondering where he was, and then smiled, matching her pace to his as they both moved downwards. Together and yet apart, drawing closer and then further away, as the oval shape of the stairs guided their separate trajectories.

She stopped halfway down and Joe followed suit, leaning against the stone balustrade that edged the well of the stairs.

'It's beautiful.' She was staring up at him and Joe nodded.

'Shame we can't stay a little longer.' A party of tourists were walking down behind him and Joe stood back to let them pass, watching as they wound their way down. Bel did the same and then they were alone again, in this delicious formal dance, which seemed so much more intimate for the distance between them.

They lingered as long as they could, and then made their way together to the bottom of the stairs. When he reached Bel she was standing in the middle of the stairwell, looking up. Joe was just in time to steady her as she stepped back suddenly, clearly finding the upward view almost as dizzying as the downward one had been.

'Steady…' He murmured the word quietly, and she leaned against him. Just for a moment, so they could both look upwards together. And then the moment was gone, as the door into the main entrance opened and an attendant appeared, clearly intent on chivvying them along before the gallery closed for the evening.

That was probably all for the best. Joe wasn't

sure how to let go of this, although he knew he must. They took one last look behind them and then they were outside, walking towards the main gates.

'What next?' Joe regretted the question as soon as he'd asked it. He didn't want to go for coffee or a meal, and talk about everyday things—that felt like a step backwards. And there was no going forward either. It was too soon when he couldn't find any words for what had just happened between them.

Bel's forehead creased in thought, and then she reached into her handbag, taking out their entrance tickets. 'I think I'd like to go home now. But the tickets are for the Galleria Corsini as well. We'd have to go within the next twenty days.'

That was…exactly what Joe wanted too. No need to talk about this just yet, but there was the promise of more. Another chance for them both to tear themselves away from the past and find a way forward.

'I'd like that.' Bel proffered one of the tickets, and Joe shook his head. 'You keep them safe.'

She nodded, unzipping one of the compartments inside her bag and stowing the tickets carefully away. This was fine. It was all good. Now all he had to do was work out how he was going to be able to tear himself away from Bel.

She appeared to have that under control as well. 'I'll see you on Monday then, at the hospital. Text me when you have some time for the Galleria Corsini.'

'I will. Maybe not next weekend, but the weekend after?' That would give them both a little time to think.

She smiled. 'I'll look forward to it.' Bel reached out as if to shake his hand, and then seemed to think better of it.

A kiss, even on the cheek, was out of the question. Joe caught her hand, his fingertips brushing hers, and she smiled up at him.

'See you later, then…'

Joe nodded. 'You can count on it.' He took a breath and then turned, not wanting Bel to feel that his gaze was still on her as she walked away. But he couldn't help looking back just once, and caught Bel doing the same. Joe raised his hand and she returned his wave.

It was a long walk home, but standing still for long enough to wait for the bus was out of the question. Joe kept up a brisk pace, wondering whether that would help him handle the feeling of excitement that tore at his heart, making it beat faster.

There was no denying it, he'd fallen a little in love with Bel this afternoon. It wasn't a feeling that Joe had any experience of—his relationships had never included any possibility of love. Mutual attraction, yes. Along with an understanding that there were no strings attached, which allowed a parting that morphed effortlessly back into friendship. Love had always been out of the question.

He'd left London because he couldn't handle the constant reminders of his parents, and come to Rome to distance himself from his grief. That had worked, and he'd built a new life here, compartmentalising the pain of having to part with them. If he fell in love now he had to be sure, and Joe knew that Bel did, too. They both needed a little time.

Still, the promise of a ticket to the Galleria Corsini warmed his heart. He and Bel weren't done with each other yet.

CHAPTER SIX

IT HAD BEEN an odd week. Bel had seen Joe at the hospital, working with him on a number of different cases, but neither of them had mentioned the Palazzo Barberini. It was still there, though, a secret pleasure for them both to keep. Something had changed and, despite all of her fears, all the resolutions that she could do without another relationship, the sweetness of those moments with Joe just wouldn't go away.

Maria's greeting when she turned up at the clinic the following Saturday was a little different from usual. 'Bel, have you heard from Joe this morning?'

'No. Should I have?'

'We were hoping you had. We've been worried about him. He was so very tired yesterday he even snapped at me, although he apologised afterwards.'

'There was an emergency at the hospital on Thursday. We were operating for most of the night, and I stayed and managed to get some sleep afterwards. Joe went home and I wouldn't be surprised if he went on straight to the clinic…'

Bel frowned. Joe always worked hard, but he pushed himself to the edge of exhaustion sometimes.

Maria frowned. 'I thought as much. I wish he'd take a day off every now and then, he's not doing himself any good. I've tried to call him but he's not answering his phone. I don't suppose you could go and see what's happening? Max says that he and Aurora will take over the new patients you were going to see this morning.'

Maria had obviously thought about this, and made a few amendments to this morning's schedule. That was fair enough. Bel was worried too. When he wasn't working, Joe's phone never went unanswered.

'Okay. What's his address?'

Maria raised an eyebrow. She knew everything that went on in the clinic and it was impossible that she could have missed that Joe had been leaving with Bel more often than not over the last few weeks. Clearly, she'd seen only their increasing intimacy and underestimated their mutual caution.

'Here…' She consulted her computer screen and wrote down the address. 'You know where that is?' If she suspected anything, then Maria had obviously decided to play along.

'Uh…yes, I think so. Down to the end of the road and turn right. It's somewhere on the left…?'

'Second on the left.' Maria gestured that she should hurry up. 'See if you can talk some sense into him, and call me. I'll call you if he turns up here…'

Joe was probably just tired and had overslept. Bel half expected to bump into him on the fifteen-minute walk to his place, and kept an eye out for him in the busy street, and in the pavement cafés where he might have stopped for coffee. But when she reached the address that Maria had given her and looked up, the curtains covering the folding doors that led out onto the third-floor balcony were closed.

She pressed the bell. No answer. Pressed it again, forgetting to take her thumb off. Still nothing. Bel wondered if anyone else in the block was at home and might let her in.

'What?' She heard his voice from the balcony above, bleary and annoyed, and stepped back so that Joe could see her. He was wearing a pair of loose-fitting sweat shorts and a sleeveless vest that left less to the imagination than usual, and Bel suppressed a smile. She'd been thinking about what his body might look like, and the promises made by the way he filled out his work clothes were more than fulfilled.

'Sorry... I must have overslept.' When he'd seen her, his annoyance had morphed into remorse. He hadn't got to embarrassment yet, and hopefully he wouldn't for another few moments.

'You look terrible.' Bel fired the accusation up at him. That wasn't entirely true, but his face was drawn and his eyes still bleary and a little swollen from sleep.

'Thanks. I'll go get a shower and be at the clinic in half an hour...'

That was an obvious invitation to leave. *'Oh, no, you don't, Joe.'* She muttered the words and he planted his hands on the rail of the balcony, leaning forward.

'What was that?'

'You're not working today.' She saw him shake his head, dismissing the idea, and switched into Italian. 'You want to discuss it? I've got all morning. We can discuss it. Right here and now...'

That did the trick. If Joe's body didn't embarrass him, and why on earth should it, then the idea of a spirited discussion from his balcony, which his neighbours would not only hear but understand, clearly did. He disappeared for a moment, and she heard the door release buzz.

By the time she'd climbed three flights of stairs, Joe had pulled a sweatshirt over his head and unsuccessfully tried to flatten his hair. If he thought that made him look any less delicious, then that was an unusual lapse in judgement. He led her through into a small, neat kitchen where coffee was brewing in a moka pot on the stove.

'Sorry, I didn't manage to grab any sleep on Thursday night, and yesterday was a busy day at the clinic. I'll be there…' He turned as the moka pot emitted a gurgling sound, seeming a little at a loss. Clearly, he was a little too drowsy to speak and make coffee at the same time.

'And what are you going to do at the clinic? Make mistakes for everyone else to put right?' She nudged him out of the way, turning the heat down under the pot and flipping open the nearest overhead cupboard, which contained a couple of espresso cups. She poured the coffee, handing one to him.

'I'll be okay when I've had coffee…'

'Oh, really?' Bel watched as Joe drank it down. 'You're okay now, are you?'

'And a shower.' He frowned at her. 'I won't be a minute.'

Bel glared back at him. 'I'll wait here, shall I?'

'Go and sit down.' He motioned towards an arch at the far end of the kitchen and turned back towards the door.

She took a seat in the sitting room. Joe's apartment was compact but it was well decorated and very tidy, presumably because he didn't spend enough time here to make much of a mess. It was noisy, though, set on one of the main roads into the centre of the city, and the windows rattled every now and then as a heavy lorry drove past. How he ever managed to sleep was a mystery, and Bel supposed that hitting the pillow with your eyes already closed was something of an advantage.

She took her phone from her handbag and texted Maria to let her know that Joe was okay but very tired, and he could do with the weekend off. Maria texted back almost immediately, saying that everything was under control at the clinic and if she saw Joe there she'd give him a piece of her mind.

Ten minutes later he appeared in the doorway of the sitting room, freshly shaved and showered and wearing a pair of casual trousers with a crisp blue shirt. He smelled sweet and cool, like gelato on a hot day.

'Ready to go?'

'No. Not yet.' She pointed towards the armchair which stood opposite hers, and Joe puffed out a breath and sat down.

'What is this, Bel? I overslept. I'm sorry that you were worried enough to come round and see whether I was okay, and I appreciate it.'

'When was the last time you took a day off? I know you haven't in the last three weeks.'

'There's been a lot to do, keeping thc place going while the basement's been out of action…' He pressed his lips together as if the answer didn't satisfy him any more than it did Bel. 'About six months. When the clinic first opened, I was working all the hours just to get it up and running. I knew I couldn't keep that up and so I made a rule for myself, to take Sundays off. Then we started to get really busy…' He shrugged.

'You need some time off, Joe. You can't keep going like this, and you really don't need to. There are people at the clinic who'll step in and take some of the weight.'

Joe shook his head. 'They're all volunteers. I don't like to ask too much of them.'

'I got there at ten this morning. By that time, you'd already been missed and I had nothing to do because Max and Aurora had shared my work out between them. We *are* volunteers and in return for that you need to allow us the right to care about the place enough to step in and help, if that's what we want to do.'

He puffed out a breath, leaning wearily back in his seat. Joe really did need some time off—he didn't seem to have either the will or the strength to fight her.

'I know it's hard to trust other people with something you've built. Especially for you.' There were times when Joe hadn't come too far from the kid who couldn't trust anyone, and letting other people take care of his dreams for a while seemed an impossible thing to ask.

'You're right. Of course.' His eyes flashed a warning, just in case she was rash enough to think that he was going to capitulate entirely. 'I don't like it…'

'No one's asking you to. But if you continue like this, you're going to make a mistake. It's okay to order one too few pots of paint, but what if you make a mistake with a patient?'

'That's not fair, Bel. When have you seen me turning up for work when I'm not fit for purpose? And don't even try to tell me that the other night was the first all-nighter you've ever done.'

'Never. And no, it's not my first all-nighter and it won't be my last. But you *know* you have to take time off—you made that resolution once. Make it again, before…' Bel stopped herself before she got into the tearful phone call from her mother, on the evening her father had collapsed and been taken by ambulance to the cardiac unit of the hospital. 'Before it's out of your hands.'

'As it was with your father?' Joe might be weary, but he still didn't miss much.

'Yes. He says now that slowing down was the

best thing he's ever done, but it was a hard way to have to do it.'

He nodded. 'No puppies. And I'm going to call Maria, because… I'm just going to call her.'

'Of course you are. And I wouldn't inflict your lifestyle onto a poor helpless puppy. I'll make some more coffee…'

Bel could hear Joe on the phone, from the kitchen. Maria was obviously giving him a piece of her mind, because the conversation consisted of long silences on Joe's part, peppered by the odd '*Va bene*, Maria.' He managed to get a few questions in about some urgent things that needed to be done today, and Bel took the opportunity to inspect the contents of his refrigerator, which didn't take long at all.

When she carried the coffee through into the sitting room, he brought the conversation to a close and ended the call. Then he puffed out a breath. 'I thought that Maria was going to be far nicer to me than you were…'

Bel chuckled. 'Never underestimate a woman on a mission. I *could* be a great deal sterner, if you want.'

'Don't be. Winning gracefully is an art.' He reached for his coffee, and downed it in one. 'So…now that I have the whole weekend off, do you have any ideas about what I should do with it?'

'We'll take a walk down to the market, maybe stop for something to eat, and then on to the supermarket. Then I'll cook for you.'

He chuckled. 'You're going to take the comfort food route?'

'No, I'm taking the putting something into your fridge, so that you eat for the next week route. Do you ever cook?'

'I cook. When I have the time.'

'Right then. We've got the time this weekend.'

Maybe this was his best life. If Joe had woken half an hour earlier, he would have gone to the clinic and brushed Maria's objections aside. But Bel wasn't so easy to ignore. There was a vulnerability about her forthright concern for him, and an understanding of his own helplessness in breaking away from the obsessions of his childhood. She got to him, in a way that was sometimes frightening but always held a dash of delight.

Rome was theirs for the day. They could wander wherever they wanted, and if Joe looked at his watch a few times, that was only out of habit. They shopped and then cooked, and he fell asleep on the sofa for an hour. When he awoke and walked through into the kitchen, he found Bel perched on a stool, reading. She laid her book aside and waved his apologies away.

He could feel the stress beginning to lift, floating away in the warmth of the evening air, when they went out to spend an hour watching the world go by. And they talked, about nothing and everything. Bel seemed to sparkle in the lights of the city, and when she left him alone, with a promise that she'd be picking him up early tomorrow, the small apartment felt suddenly lonely. Ignoring the ever-present hum of traffic, Joe fell asleep thinking only of Bel. The woman who'd come for him, ignored all of his protests, and saved him anyway.

CHAPTER SEVEN

BEL HAD TORN herself away from Joe, knowing that last night's sleep hadn't been enough and he needed to sleep again tonight. Wanting to stay with him, and watch over him as he slept, but knowing that she'd never be able to confine herself to just that. Joe was getting under her skin, and however much she tried to stop it, she couldn't.

All the same, she made her preparations for tomorrow, texting her neighbour Costanza to ask if it was all right for her to pop in, and receiving an invitation to keep her company since her young son Nico was in bed and asleep. In exchange for a promise to sit with Nico for an evening next week, and a packet of almond biscuits, Bel received a map and the loan of Costanza's car on Sunday.

She arrived outside Joe's flat bright and early, slipping into a parking spot before anyone else had the chance to take it. When she rang the bell, he appeared on the balcony.

'We're going out?' He grinned down at her, which entirely made up for the fact that he was fully dressed this morning.

'Yes. How did you know?' She'd meant this to be a surprise.

'You're dressed for walking. And holding a map. Do I need to bring a pair of trainers?'

'Yes, you'll need them.' Bel decided that giving away this much was a wise precaution.

Joe disappeared, and Bel looked down at her outfit. A summer dress wouldn't have told him anything, even if she had spent longer than usual choosing it this morning, but she supposed that her rubber-soled canvas pumps might have given the game away. She stowed the map away in the glove compartment of the car, so that he couldn't gain any more clues from it.

When Joe joined her, he looked the same as ever—downright delicious. He got into the car, twisting around to see the child seat in the back.

'This is your car?'

'No, it's my next-door neighbour's. I promised Costanza I'd look after her son while she goes out for the evening, in return. I think I got the best part of the deal. I sit with him when she goes out shopping sometimes, and he's a delight. Nico is autistic and the supermarket tends to put him into sensory overload.'

Joe nodded. 'I guess that being right next door is handy for both of you.'

'Yes, Costanza has her mum and several other trusted friends who'll look after Nico, but sometimes she just needs to pop out for half an hour. She was a tour guide before she had Nico, and she's given me a strict itinerary for this morning.'

'And you're not going to let me in on that yet?'

Bel shot him a smile. 'No. Not yet.'

She parked in the car park that Costanza had suggested, and Joe took the small day pack she'd brought from her shoulder, insisting that he carry it. When they got onto the bus, to take them the rest of the way to the Via Appia Antica, he must have realised where they were going, but said nothing.

'Have you been here before?' Bel asked as they walked past the visitor centre, along a paved route that was more than two thousand years old, and connected Rome to Brindisi.

'Never got around to it.' Joe was obviously pleased that he had now, and set off at a jaunty pace, leaving Bel to run to catch up with him.

The National Park was closed to traffic on Sundays, and if it hadn't been for the other walkers and cyclists it would be easy to imagine that they were travelling out of the city and back in time. They spent a couple of hours exploring, stopping to see villas, basilicas, aqueducts and tombs along the way, and then sat down for a while to rest and enjoy brunch from the backpack, surrounded by rolling countryside.

'This is wonderful.' Joe flopped onto his back on the grass, his eyes closed, letting the sun warm his face. 'It feels like a different world...'

That was exactly as Bel had hoped. She'd wanted to take him away from the everyday for a while, and allow Joe to experience the feeling that there were other worlds, other ways of existing. She felt it too, that here it was possible to see beyond the people and things that had moulded her life.

'There's a lot more to see. This park stretches for more than ten miles.'

'It would be a shame to rush it and miss anything. We'll have to come back.'

Maybe one day soon, along with the local people who brought picnics on a sunny Sunday and were almost as numerous as the tourists who wanted to walk or cycle the Appian Way. Bel nodded.

'What happens to it after it leaves the park? On its way down to Brindisi?' Joe asked, rolling onto his side and propping himself up on one elbow.

'Costanza says it varies. In places it's covered by roads and buildings, and in other places it emerges and you can walk it. She says that in some places they're digging down to find it and bring it back.'

He nodded. 'It's amazing. I can't help thinking of all the toil and suffering that's gone into this place, as well as the magnificence of the achievement.'

All brought together by the passage of the years. There was a lesson here, for both of them, in the peace of this sunny morning but Bel couldn't quite bring it into focus.

'I suppose that's life, isn't it? Never quite one thing or the other.'

'Yeah. I suppose so.'

Instead of exploring any further, they decided to take their time in walking back and taking a second look at the things they'd already seen. But Joe marked their progress on the map that was spread out between them on the grass, smilingly telling Bel that this was for the next time they visited. That was more than enough for one morning.

The park had worked its magic on both of them, and there was suddenly no reason why Bel shouldn't ask Joe in for coffee when she parked Costanza's car back in its regular spot, after stopping to fill the petrol tank. Then she unlocked the door that led to the small courtyard, around which the three-storey block of apartments was arranged. Costanza was in the courtyard, watching Nico play, and Joe hung back, giving Costanza a cheery wave as Bel went to talk to the boy and return the car keys.

'This is nice.' They climbed the steps up to the third-floor walkway, lined with pots of flowering plants and herbs, and Bel stopped outside the sliding doors that led into her sitting room. 'It's hard to believe we're in the centre of the city, here.'

'Yes. The rent's very reasonable, because the landlord's selective about his tenants. No wild parties or sub-letting…' Bel bit her tongue. She could have just agreed with him, but instead she'd allowed a streak of defensiveness into her response.

Joe chuckled. 'You're not living in any more luxury than you can afford on a doctor's salary, then.' His grin told her that he was teasing, but it still hurt a little.

'No, actually. I'm not. I just took a bit of time in finding somewhere nice to live.'

'Point taken. I should do the same, my apartment's a bit noisy.' He shot her a querying look as Bel huffed at him.

'I'm not making any points, Joe. I don't have to justify everything I do in terms of whether or not my father's helped me out.'

He kept his cool. Maybe Bel should take a leaf

from his book and simmer down—her own preoccupations were beginning to show. 'I meant that I'd taken the point with regards to my own lifestyle. What you do is entirely up to you.'

Suddenly everything was okay again. Bel laughed, unlocking the door and sliding it back. Joe stepped inside, then made a show of looking around and shrugging dismissively. The magic of the Via Appia still remained, and they could still look back and see the roads they'd already trodden as different from the road ahead.

'Can't you find somewhere else?' Joe must have a good salary from the hospital, even though he only worked four days a week. Bel suspected that she knew where all of his spare cash had been going.

'I've been thinking about it. The money I'd put aside for a deposit came in handy when we needed to dry the basement out. The clinic couldn't afford all of it.'

'Just as well I managed to get a good price, then.' She reproached him, 'You'd be living on the streets.'

He chuckled. 'Not on the streets. I might have been sleeping under my desk in the office. Or there's actually a small loft living space at the clinic. We did think of raising some cash by doing it up and letting it out, but there's no separate entrance and we couldn't get the relevant permissions. It's done a few of the volunteers a good turn, though. Max stayed there for a while a couple of months back when he split up with his girlfriend.'

'Living above the clinic would be a bad idea though, wouldn't it.' Joe would struggle to take ten minutes off, let alone a whole weekend.

'Yeah. Suppose so.'

She wouldn't put anything past Joe, in his determination to make sure the clinic survived. But maybe now wasn't the time to raise the issue of whether he really should be giving this much, when there were other ways of handling the clinic's problems. Today was supposed to be the time when they could take a short holiday from all of that.

'Are you hungry?' After a morning spent walking in the open air, Bel reckoned that Joe would be as ready for something to eat as she was.

He nodded. 'Since you insisted on cooking for me yesterday, then today you can drink cocktails or read a book—whatever floats your boat—and let me cook for you.'

'All right.' Watching Joe cook was actually the thing that would really float her boat… 'I think you'll find my fridge is a little better stocked than yours was.'

'Yeah.' He shot her a grin. 'Of course it is…'

* * *

Today had been just perfect. Joe was well aware that Bel had put some effort into making it so, but he knew that he'd contributed something too. The chemistry that sparked between them had blossomed into fire, when they'd both allowed it a little time to do so. All it had taken was an unspoken agreement to set aside the past.

That couldn't last. But for now it could be enjoyed, like an exquisite flower that bloomed only for one day. They'd cooked together, and eaten together. And then, with nothing else to do, they'd watched an old black and white movie, chosen from Bel's collection of films.

'That was…predictable.' Joe had taken the liberty of putting his arm on the sofa cushions behind her shoulders, since Bel had taken a similar liberty in moving close during a particularly tense scene, and never moved away again. He'd spent the second half of the film taking more notice of her scent and the warm feel of her body than what was happening on the screen.

'That's why I like old films. You tend to know who the villain is.'

From what she'd told him, Bel knew all about villains. Although the one who had hurt her had managed to conceal his true nature. Joe was just wondering whether she might have a type, and he could be classified as a villain, when he felt her move against him.

'Thank you for today. I really needed a break, too.'

He felt her lips against his skin as Bel kissed his cheek. She lingered a little too long for that to be a gesture between friends, and Joe's hand shook as he reached up to run his finger gently along her jaw.

They could stop now. Pretend that this was just a show of affection on a lazy Sunday afternoon. If they wanted to, they could stop right now. But then Joe's gaze found hers and it was too late.

All the same, he hesitated. He gave Bel every opportunity to draw back and make coffee, or find another film, or whatever else might defuse the sudden heat between them. But when he ran his thumb gently across her lips in a gesture that might signify an end, even though that was the very last thing on his mind, he felt her hand on his wrist, keeping it right where it was so that she could kiss his fingers.

'Is this a good idea, Bel?' At least there was no longer any question over what was going on between them, and he could ask.

'No, I think it's a terrible idea.' She leaned forward, kissing his cheek again.

'And…so you think we should stop?' Joe caressed her cheek.

'You want to?'

'No. I don't.'

'Neither do I.'

Her admission broke him. He wound his arms around her, and pulled her close. There was one exquisite moment before their lips met, a chance for Bel to pull away from him, which he knew now that she wouldn't take. Joe kissed her with all the tenderness he could muster, and she responded fiercely. He kissed her again, this time taking all that he wanted, and heard her gasp.

He could feel her flesh burning under his touch. He'd never wanted a woman so much before, never felt that what happened next was a matter of life or death. If he was going to take all that he needed right now, then he had to be sure.

'What would the clinic's biggest donor say if he knew what I was about to do with his daughter?' The question was deliberately intended to pour cold water over their desire, but Joe realised that a bucket of water was little use against a rapidly spreading inferno.

'It's none of his business.' Bel moved away from him, trapping him in the warmth of her gaze. 'Anyway, what do you want more? Me or the clinic?'

Right now, the clinic could fend for itself.

But tomorrow things might be different, and Joe wouldn't take what he wanted by giving Bel false promises.

'You won't like my answer...'

She smiled suddenly. 'It's honest and I like that very much. I don't have any promises to give you, Joe, and I know you don't have any for me. But we could spend the rest of the afternoon showing each other that things could... just might...be different.'

'That's something I *can* believe in.'

Her laugh sounded like pure joy. Something not yet tamed by any of the awkward realities of life. Bel pulled away from him, stepping back a couple of feet, her fingers straying to the top button in the line that stretched down the front of her dress.

She was going to let him watch her undress. The thought was exquisite, but there was something he wanted even more. Joe got to his feet, drawing her against him. He knew she must be able to feel his arousal, and she melted against him, letting out a sigh.

They were both ready for what came next, but this was far too precious to rush. He tipped her chin up, and her gaze met his.

'Look at me, Isabella...' He'd never used her full name before, but now it seemed appropriate. More beautiful, and a mark of his respect for her.

'What are you going to do, Joe?'

Making that clear to her was all part of the pleasure. 'I want you to leave the buttons to me. Just let me see your face.'

She smiled, stretching her arms up and wrapping them around his neck. He backed her slowly until the wall stopped them, and then reached for the top button, his hand skimming her breast as he did so. Bel gasped, but never took her gaze from his as he undid the button carefully, sliding his fingers across the skin beneath it.

'There are at least twenty...'

That sounded a lot like a challenge. Joe undid three more, and found the soft, silky material that covered her breasts. His hand could explore a little more now, and he could see from her reaction that it pleased her. She pressed her hips against his, smiling as he struggled to maintain their naked eye contact.

'Are you going to last as long as twenty? There may be more, I'm not sure,' Bel teased him.

'I can if you can.' That sounded a lot like a promise, but it was one he wasn't afraid to give.

Buttons were important. Cheap buttons could ruin an outfit, and changing the buttons on a piece of clothing could lift it from ordinary to exclusive. But Joe could turn them into a countdown of desire.

He wasn't afraid to change the pace, driving her to the very edge and then pulling her back, so they could explore a little more. And he was there for her, sharing his own pleasure as freely as he enjoyed hers. There was an honesty about his lovemaking that released Bel from the fears that Rory had left in her heart.

Finally, he slipped the dress from her shoulders, letting it fall to the floor. 'Bedroom?'

'Yes. Bedroom.'

He kissed her as she propelled him towards her bedroom door. She tugged at his shirt, pulling it over his head, and he finished undressing hurriedly. The time for slow appreciation was gone now, and he lifted her up, laying her back down on the bed.

'You have condoms?' he asked.

'What would you do if I told you *no*?' Bel meant to tease him, but Joe didn't miss a beat, removing her underwear and letting his fingers and tongue stray across her body, moving downwards.

'I have condoms… They're in… Oh!' His hand slipped between her legs before she could finish the sentence.

Joe grinned up at her. 'Too late. Did you think I wouldn't finish what we started?'

Not for one moment. She gave herself up to him, letting him do whatever he wanted. He was focused entirely on her pleasure and their journey here had already told him exactly what turned her on. Her orgasm seemed to have a mind of its own, unstoppable and relentless, leaving her trembling in his arms.

'They're in the second drawer down. By the bed…' She waved her hand towards the bedside cabinet.

'Now?'

Desire was still surging inside her, still pushing her on. 'I want to feel that again. With you, this time.'

He didn't need to be told twice. Joe reached across, flipping the drawer open to fetch the box of condoms. She took him by surprise, rolling him over onto his back, and then he was all hers. Trembling as she took her time over rolling the condom down into place. Gasping as she straddled him, slowly letting him inside her.

'Isabella…'

'I like it when you call me that. Tell me what you want, Joe.'

He took her hand, pressing it to his lips. 'I want to be able to see you. You're so beautiful.'

Weren't those the words that any woman wanted to hear? But Joe really meant them. She felt him swell inside her as she moved, saw his eyes darken with desire. Bel tried to go slow, but there was no denying either of them now. She came first, the orgasm rolling over her like warm water this time, a long and easy road towards completion. Joe must be able to feel its slow pace, because he was clearly holding back and letting it run its course, but Bel knew he couldn't resist her for much longer. She knew just how to move against him and he let out a cry, clamping his hands around her hips, his body arching beneath her. She felt him pulse inside her, and then suddenly they were both reaching for each other. He took her in his arms, and she felt the heat of his skin, the wild beat of his heart.

Their lovemaking seemed to have robbed him of everything but the desire to be close to her. It was the most intoxicating feeling of all and Bel cradled him in her arms, feeling her own body relax along with his.

'You want to sleep now?' They could pull the light bedcovers over themselves and sleep together until the morning.

Joe looked over at the clock which stood on the bedside table. 'I could rest for a while. But it's only five o'clock, we still have the whole evening left.'

Bel supposed she shouldn't take anything for granted. Maybe this was a one-time thing that chemistry had dictated they both needed to do before they could move on. 'We could go out and eat?'

'We could.' Joe didn't sound any more enthusiastic about the proposal than Bel felt. 'Or we could stay here if you want.'

'And play a little more?' Her smile must have given her away, because Joe chuckled.

'Yeah. And play a little more...'

Joe's father hadn't gone into the whys and wherefores of sex all that much, but he'd given him one valuable piece of advice. Always respect a woman. Maybe he'd broken that golden rule this evening—several of the things that he and Bel had done together during the course of the evening didn't seem entirely respectful. But then she'd initiated most of them, and they'd given both of them a great deal of pleasure.

It was a reflection of the relationship that had grown up between them over the last month. They challenged each other, sometimes pushed each other out of their comfort zones. But if that worked for them and was reflected in the way they made love, then wasn't that simple honesty? Joe reckoned that was the greatest mark of respect of all.

He rolled the idea around in his head for a while, staring at the ceiling while she dozed in his arms. It was still early enough for her to throw him out, if she wanted to, and he could walk back to his apartment and sleep alone.

When she stirred against him, he realised that he needed to ask.

He phrased the question as carefully as he could. 'What we did together was amazing. Mind-blowing—' She opened her mouth to reply and he laid his finger across her lips. 'I will promise you one thing. I won't speak of this afternoon unless you speak of it first. But I'll always remember it.'

'Have you quite finished?' She poked her finger into his ribs. That was probably a good sign.

'No, not really. I could elaborate…' He kissed her cheek, feeling Bel snuggle against him.

'On how this isn't going to make any difference at all to anything?' He could feel her lips moving against his skin as she spoke, and it was uniquely delicious. 'I don't want to hear it.'

'It made a difference.' Bel had turned his world upside down, and nothing was the same. However hard it was to admit it.

She sat up suddenly, throwing the bedcovers back. 'I rather liked it.'

It was very difficult to have a discussion with a woman as perfectly beautiful as she was when she was entirely naked. If Joe was ready to give her up to fond memories, then his body, still revelling in satiated pleasure, was undoubtedly sending a different message.

'I liked it. A lot.'

She leaned over to kiss him. 'You don't have to spend time wondering when the other shoe's going to drop, Joe. Whatever happens next is up to you and me, and you can trust me to tell you what I want.'

The years of never being sure of anything but himself had left their mark, but maybe they *could* both learn to live their best lives. Maybe even together, although that seemed like a challenge.

'I meant it when I said that I'd be taking a bit more time off in the future and…' He shrugged. 'We're still busy people. But Sundays could be just for us from now on. And evenings…'

Bel nodded her agreement. 'Public holidays?'

He reached for her, pulling her down next to him. 'Definitely public holidays.'

She kissed him. Joe allowed himself the possessive pleasure of rolling on top of her, in a promise of what was suddenly still possible between them, and she reached up to caress his cheek.

'You have a deal, Joe. Will you stay with me tonight? I'd like you to.'

'I'd love to. I can get up early and walk back over to my place for a change of clothes. After I've made it clear that I'll be seeing you later, of course.'

'I'll look forward to it. In the meantime, I

don't suppose you'd like to take me out for pizza, would you? I'm really hungry and it's still only nine o'clock. There's a nice place just around the corner from here.'

Joe chuckled, getting out of bed. 'Pizza would be great, I'm hungry too. Only I may need to shower first.'

'Me too. If we do it together, it'll save water…'

CHAPTER EIGHT

DESPITE ALL THEIR DIFFERENCES, there was one thing that they both agreed on. Neither Bel nor Joe was in love.

Enjoying spending time together was absolutely fine. Honesty was more than fine. It was the thing that held them together. Feeling that they'd turned each other's worlds upside down was good too—it was all part of the best life project. Love was a dangerous commitment, a step too far that neither of them was willing to take. If something went unacknowledged, then wasn't it like a leaf falling in a forest, with no one to see or hear it? How could it exist, let alone change their lives?

That didn't seem to hold Bel back, though. When Joe left the hospital on Monday evening, bound for the clinic, he found that she was walking beside him, her hand in the crook of his elbow.

'This is nice. But don't you want to go home?' During the few hours they'd been apart, a seed of longing for Bel had already begun to grow in his heart. Joe had resolved to ignore it, because there were things he had to do this evening.

'Are you?'

'No, I have a couple of patients to see, and then I need to check on the new flooring in the gym, and see how that's going.'

'Two patients and looking at a floor won't take long, will it?'

'No, but…' There were probably quite a few other things that would claim his attention and fill the whole evening, but Joe couldn't call them to mind. 'You're not taking me in hand, are you? Because I'm quite capable of organising my time.'

She laughed. 'I wouldn't dream of it. You've held down a job and built a clinic in the last three years. That's an achievement in terms of time management, if ever there was one.'

He stopped walking, looking around the crowded pavement. 'There's a *but* heading my way, I'm sure of it. I just can't see it yet.'

'No, there isn't.' Bel shot him an exasperated look. 'I know you have commitments, Joe. I can walk with you from the hospital to the clinic though, can't I? It's more or less on my way home.'

That was a challenge he hadn't anticipated. It was heart-warming to find that Bel was willing to snatch this time with him as he hurried from one task to another, but it wasn't really fair. And she couldn't disentangle him from the mass of jobs and responsibilities that the clinic provided—only he could do that.

By Wednesday he'd admitted that maybe he'd become a little bogged down in tasks that he could leave to others. On Friday he'd asked Maria whether she might consider coming in at four o'clock instead of six for a while, to oversee the repairs, and she'd jumped at it. She and her husband were planning a trip next spring and she could do with the extra money.

On Saturday Bel had spent the morning at the clinic, and Joe had promised to be at her place shortly after six, when the clinic closed. He'd left at six o'clock sharp, leaving Maria to lock up, and found himself hurrying to meet her. Bel had buzzed him in, and was waiting at the front door for him, ready to fling her arms around his neck.

'That's nice.' He disentangled himself from her kisses. 'What did I do to deserve this?'

'You kept your promise.'

That hadn't been difficult. He'd been thinking about this evening, and the prospect of another Sunday spent with Bel, for the whole week.

'Did you think I wouldn't?'

She shrugged, turning away from him and walking into the kitchen. She'd been preparing something, and a covered dish stood on the top of the cooker, ready to go into the oven. Bel opened the wine cooler, taking out a bottle and showing him the label. Joe nodded without even looking at it, and she fetched a pair of glasses. Her movements seemed somehow jerky, and strange.

'Hey…' He took the bottle-opener from her hand, laying it down. 'That can wait. What's up?'

'I just… I didn't want to expect too much of you.'

'I said I'd be here. Did you think I'd leave you sitting around all evening, wondering when I was going to turn up?' She probably had been, and Joe had to admit that he hadn't given her much reason to expect otherwise. He was still unsure of how a commitment ought to go, and hadn't told her that he'd been aching for some time alone with her.

She dismissed the idea with a wave of her hand. 'That doesn't matter. It didn't happen…'

'It *did*, though.' Joe hazarded a guess. 'Your father?'

She shook her head. 'No, Dad was always busy and he worked long hours. But when I was little he used to go into work early so he could be home in time to read me a story a couple of evenings a week. He probably did a few more hours in his study afterwards, but I always knew he'd be there if he said he would.'

'Who then?'

She turned the corners of her mouth down in a frown. 'It doesn't matter.'

'It obviously matters to you.' Joe took her in his arms. 'And it matters to me, too. We're both in a profession where sometimes we have to work a little late. That makes it all the more important to me that you know this. If I say I'll be here and don't turn up then it really is a matter of life or death.'

'My fiancé.' The word made Joe swallow hard. He'd known that there was *someone* but hadn't realised it had been quite that serious. 'He was always working late, never there when he said he'd be. And I'd always wait for him. When it came out that he'd been involved in fraud, I didn't believe it and I defended him. And when he implicated me…' A tear ran down her cheek.

'You didn't believe that either?'

'It was Dad who made me see it. His office has a card system that logs everyone in and out, and he ran a check on exactly when Rory had been in the building. He hadn't been working late at all, he'd lied to me.'

'Where was he?'

'I have no idea. I'm not sure that I want to know either. There *was* a woman involved in the fraud—she'd apparently turned up at the bank and signed a few things with my name. Dad took me down to his lawyer's office and they went through everything with me. One allegation after another…'

'That must have been very hard.' No wonder Bel couldn't let go of it.

'It was hard for Dad as well. He told me afterwards that he was wondering if I'd ever speak to him again, but he'd reckoned that I had to know the whole truth, in order to defend myself.'

'But you did. Speak to him.'

'It was touch and go at one point. I loved Rory, and he'd manipulated me into thinking that he loved me. But I knew that I couldn't blame Dad for what he'd done and, if anything, it's made us closer.' She turned her gaze up to meet Joe's. 'I can't judge you by it either.'

Joe smiled down at her. 'I don't know. If a little punctuality and letting you know if I really *am* detained at work is enough to get me into your good books…' He winced as Bel planted her hands on his shoulders, pushing him away. 'Okay. I'm hoping you see a little more in me than that.'

'Don't fish for compliments, Joe. Do you imagine that *not* being Rory is enough? That's setting the bar very low.'

He'd always been aware that he didn't have a

great deal to offer Bel. He commanded a good salary from the hospital, but most of that went on the clinic and he didn't have much left over to spend on himself or her. Her parents might not live an ostentatious life, but they'd been able to give Bel opportunities that were way beyond Joe's reach.

'Maybe I'm hoping that you do set the bar a little low, so that I can reach it.'

'Did you think that last Sunday was setting the bar low?' She reached forward, hooking her finger around one of the buttons of his shirt. Just one small gesture that set him on fire.

'Last Sunday couldn't have been any more perfect.' Joe forgot about his uncertainties and wound his arm possessively around her waist. 'And to tell you the truth, you're a great cook, and I'm sure that's a very good bottle of wine. Right now, I'd like to set the bar a little higher.'

'How are you going to do that?' She reached up, standing on her toes to kiss him.

Not the way she thought. Joe kissed her again, breaking away from her to pick up the book that was propped upside down on the kitchen counter. Bel always had a book with her, and she'd clearly anticipated his late arrival and provided herself with a little company.

'You're reading Jane Austen?'

Bel shot him a puzzled look. 'Rereading. I've read this one before, but I really like it.'

'How do you feel about going back to the beginning? Reading the first few pages together?' This was somehow more intimate than sex. Letting Bel into a world that he'd always kept for himself.

'That was about the last thing I had in mind for this evening...' She grinned up at him. 'I wouldn't have thought you'd be a Jane Austen fan.'

'I used to read a lot when I was a kid. Mostly anything I could get my hands on—it's surprising how many things you find you *do* like.'

Bel took the paperback from his hands. 'This means something, doesn't it. I'm just not quite sure what.'

If you were going to romance a girl with a book, then she needed to know what that meant. 'When I went somewhere new I'd wait a while and then ask if I could read one of the books on the shelves. Everyone used to say yes, and I'd work my way through as many as I could. Some places were four book places, others five or six...'

'Ah, I see. So there was *something* you took with you whenever you moved. You didn't tell me that.'

'I haven't told anyone. My parents figured it

out, and they started to sit down with me every evening before tea. We'd take turns to read, ten minutes each. Dad used to be really good at doing all of the voices—he had us in fits of laughter when we read *The Moonstone* together.'

'That's such a nice memory. Thank you for sharing it.' Bel reached up, caressing his cheek. 'I haven't read *The Moonstone*, but I do have loads of other books…'

'So you do.' The stacked bookshelf in the sitting room was impossible to miss. 'I'm not very good with sharing, because it gives me something to lose. But I'm sharing this with you, and in return I want you to know that I'll be here when I say I will.'

Bel hesitated, running her fingers across the cover of the paperback. It was a lot to ask of her. A lot for Joe to give. Then suddenly she pressed the book into his hands.

'Dinner can wait. Let's read, Joe.'

He picked up the bottle of wine, and Bel reached for the glasses and the bottle-opener. Then she propelled him through the sitting room and into the bedroom.

Time had gone so quickly. And yet slowly too, because Bel had been catapulted into a world where everything was new and different. They were like explorers who'd discovered an enchanted forest and—hand in hand for courage—had dared to step inside its scented canopy.

But somehow it was all right. She could make a habit of being this easy and relaxed with someone. Not just any old someone—it had to be Joe.

Last night had been very special, but they still had a way to go and Joe was stepping as carefully as she was. He hadn't taken an invitation to stay the night for granted, and they'd had to walk back to his apartment on Sunday morning to pick up a change of clothes for him. A window in the sitting room had been left ajar to let in some air, and he closed it, shutting out the noise of the traffic. Bel sat down, trying not to look around for some sign that Joe had made a home here.

'Sorry. It's not very welcoming…' Joe seemed to be seeing it for the first time.

'How long have you been here?'

'Since I first arrived in Rome. I thought I'd stay for a couple of months and look around for something nicer, but I never got around to it. I'm not here all that much, and it suits its purpose.'

What purpose would that be? Not having anything that looked too much like home, so that it wouldn't hurt to lose it? Bel decided not to ask.

'My landlord mentioned that an apartment in my block was going to be free soon…'

He smiled. 'Say what you mean, Isabella. You called him and asked, didn't you?'

Bel glared at him. 'I happened to call and he happened to mention. That's as far as I'll go, if you're going to interrogate me about it.'

Joe nodded. 'I imagine the deposit will be a lot more than I'll get back on this place. They don't have any difficulty in finding tenants, do they?'

'No. I put my name down for a place there as soon as I knew I was coming to Italy and I was lucky to get my apartment so quickly. I could put a word in with the landlord though, he might well agree to letting you pay part of the deposit later. His primary concern is getting good tenants, he says that's worth a lot…'

Joe walked over to the sofa, sitting down next to her. When he put his arm around her shoulders, Bel knew she'd probably said too much.

'And this landlord. I don't suppose you happen to know him, do you?'

Bel puffed out a breath. 'He's actually my dad's friend, but he comes to the house a lot when he's in London, so I've known him since I was little. But this is business. He has several apartment blocks in Rome and I pay the going rate for rent.' She felt her spine begin to stiffen defensively.

'I didn't say that you don't. That's not quite the point, though.'

'Well, what *is* the point? Are you saying that I can't ask a family friend about finding a nice place to live?'

'Not for a moment. And you don't have to justify your actions to me.'

Joe always said that, and Bel was just beginning to believe it. But now she'd started the conversation, she couldn't let it go. 'Well, you don't have to justify your actions to me either. But I'm not at all sure that I understand you sometimes, Joe.'

'That's good. Trust me.'

'Is that supposed to be an explanation? Because I don't understand that either.' She frowned at him, pushing him away when he went to kiss her. There were some things that Joe could bat away with just one touch of his fingertips on her skin, but this wasn't one of them.

'Okay. I've just found your hard limit with regard to avoiding the subject. That's good, I'll keep it in mind.'

'Yes, do. It'll save a bit of time in future.' They might not see eye to eye at the moment, but the future was still there, holding them together. 'So what's the problem? You don't want to live in the same apartment block as me?'

He shook his head. 'I wouldn't have to walk so far for a change of clothes. I might not like this place very much, but it serves its purpose. It's close to both the hospital and the clinic, the rent's low and…' He shrugged. 'No one's done me any favours to get me here and I really wouldn't care all that much if I had to leave.'

'And that's still one of your hard limits?' After last night she'd thought it might have softened a little, but then she'd never had to leave a place she called home, nor had she ever worried about not being able to repay a favour if needed. They were privileges she'd just taken for granted.

'Afraid so. I know it must sound as if I'm being unreasonable.'

'Yes, it does if I don't think too much about it. But however much I'd like to deny it, I was born with a different set of rules than you were.'

He leaned forward, and this time Bel allowed him to kiss her. It was well worth the wait…

'That's not a bad thing. My mum and dad did their best to undo those rules, and for a while they did, but then I lost them…' He shook his head. Another hard limit. Joe never betrayed his feelings over his parents' deaths, but leaving London behind and coming here spoke for him.

'You need to do this one on your own, don't you. I get it, Joe. We don't need to do everything all at once.'

He nodded. That was the most she'd get out of him, but it was enough. His response when she kissed him again told her that.

'Are we done? Can I go and get changed now, so we can get on with our day?' They were planning to use their tickets to the Galleria Corsini today.

She closed her fingers around the material of his shirt, hanging on tight. 'No, we're not done. If you can't take any help in finding somewhere, then maybe we'll just have to find a way to stop the clinic from draining your bank account from every spare cent.'

'Okay. Not sure how we're going to manage that…' He gently disentangled her fingers from his shirt, getting to his feet. 'I don't imagine that'll stop you from thinking about it, though.'

Joe never entirely shut her suggestions down. He might reject some of her answers, but he was always open to more. They were on a journey together, where the landscape might change with every turn of the road. That was a challenge to both of them, but there was always some hope of change.

Lending him the money for a deposit was out of the question. Bel knew he wouldn't accept that. Giving him a way to make the clinic more stable financially—he couldn't turn that down and it would give him a chance to spend some of the money he earned on things that he needed.

There was a way. One that challenged Bel,

and put her directly in the firing line for anyone who wanted to judge her. She'd thought about it, though, and by the time Joe arrived at her apartment the following Friday evening she'd decided on what she was going to do.

'You're early. I'll make some coffee before we read, shall I?' She took the book that he'd picked up from the sitting room out of his hands and he grinned.

'Yeah. Coffee will be nice. What did you want to ask me?'

Joe was always one step ahead of her. Bel supposed that was only fair, since she usually knew what was on his mind. 'You could at least wait until I decide to say I have something to ask.'

'Okay. Fair enough.' He usually stayed in the kitchen to talk when she had something to do there, but now he walked back into the sitting room and sprawled on the sofa, tapping his fingers on the cushions in a show of mock impatience.

'All right. You can stop now.' She took the coffee in, setting the pot down on the table in front of the sofa. 'I've got an idea.'

'A two cup one?' Joe had picked up the Italian habit of draining a small espresso cup in one, and he set his empty cup down next to the pot. 'Go on…'

'It strikes me that the clinic needs to have a fighting fund.'

He nodded. 'Yeah, that was always the plan. We're the victims of our own success in that way—the demand for our services has always outstripped our fund-raising capacity.'

'In that case we need to think big, try and raise enough money to cover the clinic's costs for the next year. Something to give you a breathing space.'

He stared at her. 'That sounds…amazing. Is it even possible, though?'

'No, not with a few collecting boxes and a raffle. But we could organise a fund-raising evening. Mum and Dad get asked to that kind of thing all the time—they go if the charity appeals to them. They have champagne and a nice dinner.'

Joe chuckled, clearly not even reckoning this was worth thinking about. 'Sounds like a nice evening out. You do know that there are a lot of things that need doing before we can even contemplate champagne? Maria has to open a window and tell people to push hard on the entrance door…'

'Yes, I'd noticed. We can dispense with the champagne and the dinner. We are what we are. The clinic has different things to offer.'

'I won't disagree with you there. But isn't the

whole point of one of these high-class dos that you get a really nice evening out, in return for a donation?'

'Yes, it generally is. Dad always complains that he'd rather just make a donation, he can go out and drink champagne with his friends whenever he likes. But the thing is that it's really all about making contacts. Matching the right people with the right charities, and setting up a support network. I can do that, Joe. I have the contacts because I've grown up in those circles.'

'You're a doctor, Isabella.' Joe frowned. 'That's what you've chosen to be, not someone who can use their contacts for a bit of PR. When you first emailed me and volunteered to help, all I saw was a doctor who was willing to give up a bit of time to help others. That's what I, and everyone else at the clinic, values you for.'

'I appreciate you saying that.' Joe had immediately put his finger on the thing that was difficult for her.

'I mean it. We're not going to compromise on that.'

'It's up to me whether I want to compromise or not, and I'm a pragmatist. There's no point in my recommending specific courses of long-term treatment if the clinic's future isn't assured. And right now, it depends on you for its survival. That was okay when you were starting out, but it can't go on for ever. You owe it to the clinic and everyone who benefits from it to give it a secure future.' Bel frowned. Maybe telling Joe that the clinic needed to function independently of him was a step too far.

He thought for a moment. 'Yeah, I take your point. What you're saying makes a lot of sense, but I just don't know how we're going to get there. Our whole ethos is about helping people be what they want to be. I know you don't want to be valued for your father's money, and I understand a bit better now why that's so important to you.'

'But you're willing to agree to a fund-raising event in principle?'

He puffed out a breath. 'Yes, of course. As long as you promise me one thing.'

'Don't do that. I'm not promising you anything until I know what it is.'

'So making love to me until I can't move is out of the question, then? Too bad,' he teased her and Bel raised an eyebrow. 'I was going to ask you to promise me that you won't be stepping out of your comfort zone. I know that you could set up a glittering evening that attracts really big donors, but that's not what you're all about, and it really doesn't reflect what the clinic's about either.'

'My comfort zone has been widening a bit lately.' That was all down to Joe.

'I very much doubt we'd be having this conversation if that wasn't the case.' His face softened. 'Mine's been widening too. But we still have our limits, and I won't agree to anything that doesn't respect yours. However much money that might raise.'

Bel refilled each of their cups with coffee. She'd been concentrating on what Joe might accept, but he'd made it very clear that this was all about her. He couldn't have said anything nicer, or more encouraging.

'It'll take some ingenuity.'

'You don't think you're up to it?' A smile flickered at the corners of his mouth.

'I didn't say that. I'll have to take a few risks, and you're going to have to trust me, but I promise I'll let you know if I do find myself colliding with my limits.'

He nodded, picking up his coffee. 'Then we're done. Let me know what you have in mind, and what you want me to do.'

'I'll come into the clinic tomorrow and make a list.' Bel downed her own coffee. 'You want to read? Or I could make love to you until you can't move—that sounds like a challenge.'

He chuckled. 'I'm the last person to deny you a challenge. Let's do both.'

CHAPTER NINE

BEL HAD TOLD JOE that they had to work fast. The clinic needed money and they couldn't wait for the kind of lead-in times that were normally required to secure a date in the calendars of the rich and famous.

Her strategy involved a combination of word-of-mouth and formal invitations. She'd spent every evening of the following week on the phone, and Joe had left her to it, supplying her with food and drink when she looked as if she was flagging. Her contacts would invite their own contacts personally, and Bel would follow up with one of the colourful invitations for a dress down, early evening event which would allow people to leave early if they had another evening engagement to attend. She'd assured Joe that printing invitations was the one thing they needed to spend money on, and he hadn't told her that he'd paid for them himself.

Last weekend they'd broken their no-work-on-Sunday rule and spent the whole day replying to emails and the RSVP cards she'd included with the invitations, assuring everyone that their presence was all that was needed, and they could pop in and back out again at their own convenience.

Everyone had helped out, volunteers and patients working together to do whatever they could. The place was clean and tidy, and Maria had made sure that the workmen in the basement had finished on time. Martina had taken charge of the catering, which would consist of various people contributing a plate of party food, which would apparently all come together and make a good spread. Joe had played his part, tidying up the office, which produced a large bag of things that needed to be thrown away and a smaller pile of things he'd thought he'd lost.

He'd found a large box, and put it behind Maria's desk in the reception area, telling her to only accept one bottle of wine from everyone, and placing his own donation in for starters. The *one bottle only* rule had been undermined when Chiara and her husband added three bottles, insisting that one was from their young son, and several other people had taken it as an open invitation to spend as much as they liked on their one bottle.

And now Bel was as nervous as a kitten. She'd dressed up for the occasion, adding a heavy gold bracelet to her plain black dress, which proved the rule that one good piece of jewellery was enough, and she was pacing up and down behind the front door of the clinic.

'Hey, Isabella…' He caught her hand, bringing her to a halt. She smelled gorgeous, but then Bel always did to him, irrespective of the price of her scent.

'You look wonderful. You've already done the most important thing we set out to do. Everyone's shown what this place means to them.' Joe hadn't realised until now how much everyone had wanted to help.

'You didn't know, did you?' She smiled suddenly.

'I didn't have the time to stop and look. I have now. Whatever happens next, everyone here will succeed or fail together, and that's already more than I could have hoped for at the start.'

'What happens if no one wants to donate?'

He shrugged. 'Then it didn't work. We'll try something else.'

'I could kiss you right now…'

They'd taken care to keep their relationship out of their work lives, which had been relatively easy at the hospital, and more difficult in the family of patients and volunteers here. Joe had been wary of letting anyone know, because he hadn't been able to believe that someone like Bel would stay with him for long. But now was time for this evening to work another of its miracles. He bent, kissing her lightly on the lips.

She reached up, wiping the lipstick from his mouth. Martina and Chiara had abandoned their therapist-patient relationship for the evening and were standing at the other end of the entranceway, waiting to greet their guests, and Joe noticed that they'd both spun around, turning their backs. He wondered whether that was his prompt to kiss her again, because one kiss was never enough.

Bel smiled up at him. 'Everyone knew already…'

The doorbell rang, and she started. Joe had spent a couple of hours with some sandpaper, under Leonardo's watchful eye, and the door didn't stick any more now. Bel flung it open, and suddenly her face was wreathed in smiles.

'Uncle Edo! I'm so happy to see you!' She hugged the man on the doorstep.

'You too, Isabella. How's your father?' Uncle Edo disentangled himself from Bel's arms and stepped inside.

'He's well—he and Mum send their love. Dad wants to know when you'll be coming to London next, he misses your nights together at the opera.'

'Soon…'

'Shall I call him and tell him to insist on a date?'

Uncle Edo chuckled. 'That would be very nice of you, darling. Now, where am I supposed to go?'

'I want you to meet the clinic's founder and director first…' Bel turned, introducing them.

'Delighted to meet you. Isabella's been telling me all about this new home of hers.' Hearing Joe's name, Uncle Edo switched effortlessly to English. 'I'm very interested in finding out first-hand what you do here.'

'Thank you. It's an honour to have you here, sir.' Edoardo Rossi was the fashion designer that every woman in Italy would give her favourite handbag to have on her guest list.

'My pleasure entirely.' Uncle Edo looked round as Chiara stepped forward.

'This is Chiara Albertini. She'd like to take your coat, and explain a little about what we do here.' Bel had taken hold of Chiara's arm, presumably to stop her from curtseying.

'Thank you. Will you indulge me, Chiara, and tell me where you found your dress?'

Chiara reddened furiously. Martina had persuaded her to wear something that she'd made for herself, before her accident, and the simple dress was elevated by a riot of embroidery at the neck and cuffs.

'It's Chiara's own creation. It's beautiful, isn't it?' Chiara was clearly completely lost for words, and Bel came to her rescue.

'Indeed. Quite remarkable.'

'I had a head injury and couldn't sew. But Martina's teaching me how to do it again…' Joe had made it clear to everyone who was helping tonight that no one was expected to tell their own story, they were here solely as hosts, but Chiara seemed anxious to add some more details. 'Now that I've seen how I might be able to do it again, I don't mind wearing some of the dresses I made before. May I take your coat?'

'Thank you.' Chiara helped Uncle Edo out of his coat, putting it carefully over her arm, her fingers running along the collar in clear appreciation of the fine material. His idea of dressing down appeared to be a silk waistcoat, made from a patchwork of riotous colour. 'It seems we have something in common and I'd be fascinated to speak with you a little more.'

Chiara straightened suddenly, beaming at Uncle Edo. Another success for the evening before it had even started. Martina appeared behind her, relieving Chiara of the coat and leaving her to guide Uncle Edo through to the reception area, where there was a gallery of photographs covering all aspects of the clinic's work.

'Edoardo Rossi is your uncle?' Joe murmured to Bel as soon as they were out of earshot.

'No, but I always called him that when I was little. My mother got to know him in Milan, and when we were there on holiday we'd spend a lot of time with him and his wife. When he lost Aunt Beatrice, five years ago, he came and stayed in London with them for several months.'

'Okay. That sounds like family to me, but what do I know? Any other very good friends turning up tonight?'

'I'm hoping for a few. And that some of *their* good friends will be coming as well…' She shot Joe a mischievous smile as the doorbell rang again.

The evening was going better than Bel had expected. There were informal tours, carried out by volunteers and patients for whoever expressed an interest, and the craft room in the basement had been cleared and food and drink laid out. People had popped in and didn't seem to be in any hurry to pop back out again. The room was full, everyone chatting to each other over a glass of wine, balancing their food on paper plates. Joe was going to have to give the just-in-case speech.

She checked that he still had his notes in his pocket, receiving a grin in answer. Then she tapped a knife against an empty glass and the room fell silent. Joe stepped forward, looking so handsome that surely anyone would give him anything in return for one of the smiles that he'd been giving away for free this evening.

'Ladies and gentlemen. I want to tell you what you've done for us already this evening…'

What? She'd expected he might drop in a few asides, because they hadn't been sure if there would be enough people together at the same time to even give a speech. But he hadn't taken his notes out of his pocket.

'Our belief here is that we can try for what seems impossible. We may not make it, but sometimes it's the journey that's worth our while. Tonight, in filling this room, Isabella has shown us that we *can* achieve the impossible if we set our minds to it.'

A spontaneous burst of applause started in one corner and rippled around the room. Bel was torn between not wanting to encourage him and being captivated by the way he'd brought everyone together so effortlessly.

'We started out wanting to raise funds for the clinic and we still do. Isabella tells me that I must mention that we'll gratefully accept anything that you feel able to give, and we'll put it to good use. She's absolutely right, but… I have to tell you something. What I see when I look at this clinic are volunteers who go above and beyond what I'd ever dare ask of them. I see patients who do the same, and who return to help others in face-to-face encounter groups and internet groups…'

Bel puffed out a breath. Everything that Joe had said was right, but he might have stressed the part about raising funds a bit more.

'Isabella has brought you here tonight, asking you to accept us as we are. And you came, and have given us your valuable time. I've personally answered a lot of hard questions, which have made me think about the issues as you see them. *This* is what we value, and we thank you for being here to give us that gift.'

He grinned as an enthusiastic round of applause, from both helpers and guests, rose in the air.

'Smart man.' Uncle Edo leaned across, whispering to her in English. 'I'd be very surprised if he hasn't just doubled a few of the cheques that'll be written on the way out…'

'He's not being smart at all—it's what he believes.' It was what Bel believed as well and she couldn't help liking that Joe had said it, even if it wasn't what she'd written.

Uncle Edo nodded. 'You're the smart one, then.'

'We're just…' It was underestimating Uncle Edo to say *friends*. He could see the body language as well as anyone else. 'Don't tell Mum and Dad just yet, eh? I don't want them worrying about me.'

'As you wish. I wouldn't say they have anything to worry about, though. I'm very impressed with him.'

'Hold that thought, Uncle Edo.' Joe was making his way over to her, stopping only to shake a few hands that had been proffered in his direction. 'One of the things that impresses *me* about him is that he'll be expecting me to mention that the speech I wrote for him is still in his pocket.'

Uncle Edo smiled, waiting for Joe to join them and shaking his hand. 'Good speech.'

'*Not* the one I wrote, though.' Bel couldn't help smiling up at him.

'Sorry. I know you spent a lot of time on it and I fully intended to stick to it... But I saw everyone just staring at me, waiting for me to say something, and reckoned that if they'd broken the rules by staying, the least I could do was tell them how I really felt about that. What the clinic means.'

'Bravo.' Uncle Edo had been nodding in agreement with Joe, and now he turned to Bel to see what her answer was.

'Uncle Edo! Could you give me just a couple of minutes to actually *have* this conversation and then I'll tell you all about it?'

'Of course.' Uncle Edo held his hands up in an expression of surrender and Bel rolled her eyes. He was one of the kindest men she knew, but surrender really wasn't his style.

But at least she had Joe to herself now. She turned to face him.

'You were absolutely right. You may have cost us a bit just then, but we agreed we wouldn't pretend that we were anything other than exactly what we are. And you put it all very nicely.'

'So we're not going to have a full and frank discussion about it?' Joe looked slightly disappointed at the thought.

'No, I'm kicking myself at not having written something like that in the first place. I'd have included something to indicate that it was *you* who gave the clinic its values.'

'I would have mentioned that it was *you* who made me look beyond my assumptions. Since you have family here, I thought it was better not to. It's up to you to decide when and if you want to tell them about me.'

'Uncle Edo's already guessed, but he knows how to keep a secret. You're aware of the fact that his new collections surprise even the most well-informed fashion correspondents?'

Joe looked at her blankly. 'No, I wasn't. But I know now.' His hand found hers and gave it a surreptitious squeeze. And then they both jumped as a loud crash sounded from the drinks table.

In the moment of silence that followed, Bel heard a wail of anguish, and Chiara's voice, repeating the word *sorry*. She turned to see Chiara picking herself up from the floor next to the overturned drinks table, and the ever-watchful Martina making her way determinedly towards her. Joe had moved too, squeezing through the press of surprised people to reach Chiara, who had begun to cry.

'It's okay.' He murmured the words, quickly wrapping a napkin around the blood that was running down Chiara's arm. 'Don't worry about this—it doesn't matter. Come with me and let me take a look at your arm.'

Chiara shook her head and Joe put his arm around her shoulders, firmly refusing to take no for an answer. Martina was comforting her too, telling her that it wasn't clumsiness but all a part of her compromised ability to judge distance and position and the two of them guided her away from the mess and out of the room.

Then something marvellous happened. The wife of one of Rome's leading industrialists took off her stylish jacket, handing it to her husband, and rolled up the sleeves of her silk blouse. She started to pick up some of the bottles that had rolled onto the floor, and another of the guests stacked them carefully out of harm's way. One of the volunteers had fetched a large packet of paper towels from a cupboard, laying them down on the new non-slip rubber flooring to soak up the spilt wine. Everyone began to work together to clear up the mess and Leonardo appeared from nowhere, directing operations and warning people away from the broken glass until gloves and brushes and pans could be fetched from the cleaning cupboard.

Bel climbed onto a chair, raising her voice. 'If our guests would like to move through into the garden while we clear up…'

Several of the guests drifted out of the room, but most of them ignored her. Uncle Edo was on the phone, and impatiently beckoned her down from her perch.

'This is… I wish they wouldn't…' Bel grimaced as he put his phone back into his pocket.

'What do you expect? You make people a part of the family and then you tell them they can't help? Go and let Filippo in, will you?'

'You're going home?' Filippo was Uncle Edo's chauffeur.

'Of course not. Just let him in, please.'

There was no arguing with Uncle Edo when he was in a mood to insist and it seemed that everything was under control here, even if no one was doing what they were supposed to. Bel heaved a sigh and went upstairs, pulling the door open to find that Filippo was already on the doorstep and carrying two crates of champagne, one stacked on top of the other.

'What?' Bel stared at him.

'You know your uncle never goes anywhere unprepared, Miss Trueman.' Filippo gave her a cheery smile. 'Where do you want it, Mr Rossi?'

'Put it down here, thank you.' Uncle Edo appeared at the top of the stairs. 'And will you fetch the other ones, please.'

Filippo deposited the crates in the hallway and made his way back outside again. Bel turned to face Uncle Edo.

'What's all this?'

'I thought you might run out, so I brought a few extras just in case. I underestimated you—there was plenty for everyone, but I didn't expect that half of it would end up on the floor.'

'Chiara couldn't help it. She has difficulty in judging distances…'

Uncle Edo waved her explanations away. 'Whatever. I'm sure no one will refuse a glass of this.'

No, they probably wouldn't—it was a very fine vintage. 'They might all be leaving any minute now.' She'd already seen one of their guests walking into the small room behind the reception area to find his coat.

'You lose a few, maybe. You keep the ones you really wanted in the first place.' Uncle Edo smiled genially at the man as he emerged, his coat over his arm. 'Thank you for coming, Claudio. I look forward to seeing you again soon.'

'Yes.' Bel smiled at him. 'Thank you so much and…sorry for the unexpected turn of events.'

'Don't apologise, Isabella,' Uncle Edo whispered as their guest left. 'It wasn't Chiara's fault and if he doesn't want to drink my champagne that's his loss. Don't you want to see what your partner is doing?' He used the Italian word that implied a dance partner rather than a business partner.

Actually, no. It had never occurred to Bel that Joe wouldn't be dealing perfectly well with Chiara's injured pride along with the cut on her arm. It appeared that trusting someone, irrespective of whether they were a dance or a business partner, was finally coming naturally to her.

'He'll be managing. He'd have called me if he needed me.'

'If you say so. I'll ask Filippo to carry the boxes downstairs and we'll put the bottles on ice in the garden, ready for a toast when everyone's finished clearing up.' Filippo appeared right on cue with another two crates. 'Filippo, you brought the ice packs?'

'Yes, Mr Rossi, I packed them around the crates so the champagne's already cool.'

'Very good. Thank you. Out of the way, please, Isabella…'

CHAPTER TEN

SINCE EVERYONE WAS clearly managing without her, Bel allowed herself to join Joe in the downstairs consulting room. Chiara was sitting with Martina on the examination couch and seemed to be recovering from the shock of her miscalculation.

'Hey.' Joe grinned at her. 'What's happening out there?'

That was Joe all over. His first concern was always for his patients, and he'd acted on those unswerving values. Martina could have dealt with the cut on Chiara's arm, but Joe knew that his place as director of the clinic was with the most vulnerable person in the room.

'They haven't left, Joe. Some of them have insisted on helping clear up—I couldn't stop them. Uncle Edo came prepared, with four crates of emergency champagne in the boot of his car, and his chauffeur's setting up in the garden as we speak.'

He chuckled. 'You've got everything under control, then?'

'Me? No, I have *nothing* under control. Everyone else seems to have everything under control.'

'That's the way you've been telling me to work for the past few weeks. If you set things up in the right way, then that gives people the ability to help. How are you finding it, by the way?'

'More annoying than I thought it would be.' Bel realised that she'd automatically slipped into English to speak with Joe, and that Chiara was looking at her nervously. 'Sorry, Chiara…' She repeated everything she'd told Joe in Italian.

'So… I haven't spoilt everything?' Chiara asked.

'You heard what Bel said—you haven't spoilt a thing. If I asked a little too much of you when I encouraged you to help, then that's my fault.' Martina had clearly already given Chiara that message and Joe nodded.

'My fault, actually. I'm the one who's supposed to be in charge here.' His grin clearly questioned whether he was in charge of anything at the moment.

'If we're going to disagree over whose fault it was, I'd be disappointed if you all overlooked me. *I* organised the evening…' Bel added, and Chiara finally smiled.

'I was the one who knocked the table over.'

'You have a disability, Chiara. Accidents happen and we owed it to you to take better care of you. I can only apologise to you that we didn't.' Joe firmly put an end to the conversation. 'How do you feel about joining Mr Rossi in the garden for a moment? Just to show you're okay.'

Bel nodded. 'I'm sure he'd like that.'

Chiara hesitated shyly and Joe nodded. 'Later maybe. Stay here with Martina, and I'll go and show my face for a couple of minutes.'

A firm knock sounded on the door and he turned, opening it. Uncle Edo was carrying two paper cups with what looked suspiciously like champagne in them. He grinned round at Chiara. 'You have a visitor.'

Chiara sat up straight, beckoning Uncle Edo inside.

'How are you? I hope you do not have blood on your beautiful dress… And that you are not hurt, of course.'

'No, it was a small cut, and Dr Dixon stopped the bleeding before I even knew about it. My dress and I are both well, thank you, Mr Rossi.'

'I'm so pleased. In that case, might I persuade you to join me in a little champagne?'

Chiara shook her head. Uncle Edo handed the champagne to Bel and she passed it on to Martina, who took a sip, nodding in appreciation.

'What about some hot chocolate, Uncle Edo?' Bel suggested.

'Even better. Thank you, Isabella. May we go to the garden now and find a seat where we can talk, Chiara?'

'Yes!' Chiara slid down from the couch and took Uncle Edo's arm.

'Is he always like this?' Joe murmured as he followed Bel into the small kitchen on the first floor.

'No, he's usually worse, but he promised me he wouldn't interfere when I asked him to come.' Bel reached up for two cups from the cupboard, while Joe got milk from the fridge. 'Now you have an idea of how the Italian side of my family behaves, do you have second thoughts about me?'

He curled his arm around her waist. 'Not for a moment. A little constructive interference from friendly uncles is something I missed out on, so I'm very grateful for it now. Just as I'm incredibly grateful to you for your constructive interference in my life, even if I sometimes don't appear to be.'

Another surprise, in an evening full of them. This was the best, though. 'Are you saying that you'll do exactly as I tell you in future?'

'Of course not. Do you really want a man who doesn't put up a fight?'

'No. That would become boring...' She kissed him, and he smiled.

'That's what makes *my* evening complete, Isabella. But we need to make the hot chocolate and then get ourselves downstairs to thank each and every one of our guests personally for staying...'

The evening was supposed to run from five until seven o'clock, but no one seemed disposed to leave and the mix of patients, volunteers and guests were still out in the garden chatting at nine o'clock. Uncle Edo offered Chiara and Martina a lift home at ten, and volunteers and patients who were car-pooling started to pull on their coats as well. Joe and Bel said goodbye to the last of their guests, and when he closed the door behind them Bel fell into his arms, hugging him with relief.

'You want to go and see what's in the donations box?' He was holding her tightly, clearly as overwhelmed by the evening as she was.

'You know...actually, I'm not even sure that I care.'

'Me neither. I think we collected more than money tonight. Our people had a chance to reach out and speak about the things they've faced. And they were listened to.'

Bel nodded, snuggling against him. There *was* more at stake tonight—it was important to raise some money to ease the financial burden that the clinic placed on Joe. She enjoyed the warmth of his arms for one moment longer, and then moved away.

'We'll look. At least we won't be wondering all night, eh?'

There were some five and ten euro notes in there, presumably from those who'd taken the sound of broken glass as a cue to leave. But there were cheques as well, along with an envelope with her name on it in Uncle Edo's precise handwriting. Bel read his note, while Joe counted the cash and made a list of the amounts donated by cheque.

'Joe, read this!' She handed over the note and he scanned it. 'I told him that he wasn't to donate anything, we just needed him to be there, to lend some social prestige…'

Joe read the note. 'Six front row seats for his autumn show in Milan. Chiara to be his special guest…' He grinned. 'She'll love that. The other five seats can be auctioned off in support of the clinic. And… What's he saying in the final paragraph?'

'Fashion houses often alter clothing for very important or influential customers. Each of these six seats includes one piece of clothing from the collection, whatever the person chooses and made individually for them.' Explaining the Italian words still didn't seem to give Joe any idea of what it all meant. 'Do you *know* how valuable a gift this is?'

He shook his head. 'From the look on your face, I don't think my guess would cover it.'

'It's worth... I don't know what it's worth, to be honest. You can't buy a seat at one of Uncle Edo's shows, they're by invitation only, and for serious fashion experts with a few film stars for good measure. The front seats are the most coveted, of course.'

His brow darkened. Joe wasn't going to turn this down, was he?

'Will Chiara be all right?'

'Yes, she'll be fine. I've been in the past, but I've been too busy for the last couple of years. My mother *always* goes, though, and I'll ask her to look after Chiara, we don't need to worry about her...' Bel thought for a moment. 'You don't mind, do you? I didn't ask Uncle Edo to do this.'

Joe shook his head slowly. 'I'm a bit out of my depth with it but... How could I mind, when he's been so generous?'

'I meant do you mind that this is my family?'

He leaned over, kissing her. 'You're beautiful, a great doctor, and you have a true heart. I have no idea why you choose to spend your time with me, Isabella. But I'm very thankful that you do.'

'Don't underestimate yourself, Joe.' Bel returned his smile. 'Although if you could be a little quicker in totting up those donations, I'd be even *more* impressed with you.'

Joe nodded, rechecking the figures he'd jotted down and showing her the total. 'This will be more than enough to cover the rent and Maria's salary for the next year *and* give us a fighting fund for contingencies. That's a huge step forward. We can both concentrate on being doctors now, and I don't have to worry about whether we'll make next month's bills.'

Bel nodded. 'You deserve that, Joe. Are you going to think about putting some of your own salary aside to get a decent place to live now?'

'Yeah. I have to admit that'll be a relief as well.'

Nothing came without a price. Joe had the most beautiful woman in the world in his bed—or rather she had him in hers, because Bel's preference for the quiet of her own apartment was more than reasonable. The clinic's short-term future was secure, and he could start to consider how he might build on that. He was waiting for the other shoe to drop.

But maybe it was enough that it didn't drop on Sunday morning, when he and Bel went back to finish clearing up after the party and found that several of the volunteers had had the same idea. The work went much quicker than he'd expected, and he settled down in his office to start writing the personal notes of thanks to everyone who had come last night.

Sunday afternoon was theirs, to eat and talk and make love. Bel's yellow and white baseball boots hit the floor with a very satisfying thump, which didn't bother him at all.

He kissed her goodbye as the sun rose on Monday morning, making his way home and then on to the hospital. Her smile as they passed each other in the corridor on their way to different patients seemed a little subdued, but she was clearly busy. He was busy too. A patient with multiple injuries had just been brought in and he'd be operating on her this afternoon. But when Bel's name popped up on his phone as being free to assist, Joe couldn't help feeling a trickle of extra warmth in his veins.

She attended the short briefing session before lunch, and Joe stayed until everyone else had left, knowing that Bel would wait. She was sitting, nursing a cup of tea and lost in her thoughts.

'Penny for them?'

She glanced up at him. The troubled look in her dark eyes sent a shiver down his spine.

'Have you seen your email?'

'No.' Joe fished his phone from his pocket,

stabbing at the screen with one thumb. There was a string of new emails, the subject lines all different but *clinic* and *volunteering* featured in all of them. He dismissed the urge to open a few of them and closed the door, coming to sit down opposite Bel.

'What's going on?'

She took her phone from her pocket, opening a picture of what looked like a newspaper clipping. 'See for yourself. This was on the doctors' noticeboard this morning. I haven't looked anywhere else, but it's clearly on its way around the hospital.'

Joe shook his head. 'I don't want to see for myself, I want to hear it from you.'

The ghost of a smile hovered on her lips, but she didn't reply. Joe reached forward, clasping her hands between his. 'Tell me, Isabella. What's the matter?'

'It's… I'm being silly…'

'Let's dispense with the disclaimers, shall we? I'm going to take a guess and say that you're *not* being silly, and that whatever this is it's *not* nothing. I'd love to be able to give it the time it deserves, but we have a long procedure ahead of us and we need to get our heads straight and have something to eat before we scrub up. So please just tell me.'

Bel grinned suddenly. 'Don't pull your punches, Joe. I can take it.'

'Well, go on then. Tell me.' He heard tenderness creeping into his tone.

She heaved a sigh. 'Somehow, the gossip columns got wind of what we were up to on Saturday. I don't know how that happened, but I suppose I should have thought of it. We never made any secret of what we were doing and there are people whose job it is to keep tabs on what people like Uncle Edo are doing, and send photographers along.'

'Okay. So…what? He was photographed going into the clinic?' That didn't sound particularly salacious to Joe, but he wasn't acquainted with the complexities of dealing with the paparazzi.

'There's one of me greeting him on the doorstep, and another one of me answering the door to Filippo. They must have looked the clinic up on the internet and put together a story. "*Struggling free clinic runs out of champagne for Rome's rich and famous...*" Someone found it and they've pasted it up on the noticeboard, next to your appeal for volunteers.'

Joe frowned. 'That explains my inbox. I'll grant you that's annoying because it rather misses the point, but I'm assuming that's not what's bugging you.'

Bel shook her head. 'You updated your website and added my name to your volunteers list…'

'Yeah. You said that was okay at the time.'

'Yes, it was. I'm a doctor, and my name's on a lot of things in that capacity. But Uncle Edo's a close family friend and…' She shrugged.

'They put two and two together and named you as Isabella Trueman, daughter of Michael Trueman. Friend of Edoardo Rossi. I know you're not ashamed of your father or your friends, but that's not all there is to you.'

'I hope not.' Bel pressed her lips together. There was something more…

"Has anyone here been giving you a hard time?' Joe wondered whether it was appropriate for him to fly to her defence and demand an apology. He really wanted to, but Bel might decide she wanted to do that for herself.

'You know Dr Kemp in Urgent Care?'

'Vaguely. Young guy, a bit full of himself. Spends a lot of time schmoozing the registrar.'

'That's him. When I first arrived here he was too busy to give me the time of day, but this morning he came rushing up to me and started to congratulate me on what I'd been doing at the clinic. He told me that he had a few contacts and that he'd be happy to work with me on expanding the clinic's fundraising efforts and raising its profile.'

Joe could see how that must have hurt Bel. She was still bruised from her fiancé's behaviour. 'I hope you told him that we don't need a social secretary.'

'I said that he should email you, since you dealt with all of the volunteering. He didn't much like that, and said he'd prefer to send his details to me so that I could explain things to you and give you my recommendation.' She frowned. 'Which was a bit of an insult to you, I thought.'

Joe shrugged it off. If Dr Kemp didn't want to deal with him that was just fine. 'So what's your recommendation?'

Bel gave the offer a moment's consideration, which was more than it actually deserved. 'That's not what the clinic's all about.'

'Agreed. I'll write and tell him that. If he approaches you again—'

'I'll deal with it, Joe.'

He narrowed his eyes. 'So you're *not* going to give me the opportunity of defending you. I reckoned not.'

She smiled, reaching forward to caress his cheek. 'You get the job of making me strong. So I can defend myself.'

'Okay. I can hack that. I'll give all of these other emails to Maria to answer, saying that we'll be back to them within the week. There may be genuine volunteers there who just hadn't heard of us, but I think we need to weed out all of the sightseers.'

'The clinic does *need* volunteers, Joe.'

'Yes, it does. It needs people who are dedicated to helping our patients, not those who are attracted by the prospect of someone rich and famous walking through the door. It subverts everything we believe in, and it's an insult to the people who took us as we were and helped us on Saturday.'

'Maybe I should stay away for a little while.'

'No, Bel, don't do that, please. I saw the clinic in a different way on Saturday. It's a place of safety for everyone…' Joe struggled for the right words and finally said what he really wanted to say. 'I need you, Bel. And I will protect you.'

A tear ran down her cheek. Maybe it was what she'd been waiting to hear. 'Just keep telling me that, Joe.'

'As many times as you want me to.' He looked at his watch. 'Are we agreed? I need you to be there this afternoon as well.'

'To make me feel better?' Bel was teasing him now, and that was a very good sign.

'No, the general idea is to make my patient feel better.'

Bel got to her feet. 'In that case… Would you like me to get you a sandwich and something to drink from the cafeteria?'

'Would you? I'd like to take another look over these X-rays.'

'I'll be back in ten. We'll look at them while we eat.' Bel slung her bag over her shoulder, suddenly purposeful.

Joe had a feeling that he'd just witnessed the dropping of the second shoe, and it hadn't actually been so bad. Bel had been upset, but they'd worked things through together. Maybe he should take that as a lesson for the future.

Joe always made her feel better. They talked, sometimes they argued, but in the end they always saw eye to eye, always seemed to find a common purpose. And right now, that common purpose was in the operating theatre.

'She has a lot of injuries,' Bel noted as they finished scrubbing up together. Taken alone, none of them were life-threatening, but six broken bones and numerous lacerations of varying degree and type were devastating when taken together.

'Yeah. I heard that the fire department had to practically dismantle the car, it was right on top of her. And she's been weakened by shock and blood loss as well, so we need to keep a close eye on her. We have a good team, though.'

Joe was a good lead surgeon. He made sure that everyone knew exactly what they were doing, and his quiet, confident manner pulled them together as a team. Nurses, doctors and anaesthetists all liked working with him.

He'd identified the worst injury as the open, displaced fracture in their patient's leg. They would need to pin the bone, which had broken into three pieces, and then close the deep wound that had been made where one of the pieces had pierced the skin. It was concentrated, precise work, and operating with Joe always brought out the best in her.

'I think we can close now.' He was finally satisfied that the pieces of bone would heal correctly.

'Agreed.' Bel's one word confirmed his decision and he nodded.

'Guys…' Sofia, the anaesthetist, spoke suddenly, a shrill note of urgency in her tone, and Joe looked up at her. 'I think…'

One of the nurses let out a yelp, and Joe moved suddenly. He was quick enough to remove Sofia's hand from the gas flow control valve and wind his arm around her waist, catching her before she hit the floor.

'Tim, I don't think she's fainted. Keep an eye on her breathing…' Sofia was slumped against him, and he unceremoniously transferred her weight to the waiting arms of one of the nurses. 'Amy, I need an anaesthetist on the phone, now.

Everyone else, stand back and take a breath.' Joe sat down in the anaesthetist's chair, his gaze on the screens that monitored their patient.

'I've got Dr Meyer on the line.' Amy spoke up and Joe nodded.

'Thanks, will you put him on speaker…? Richard, I'm standing in for our anaesthetist, who's just been taken ill.'

'So I gather. We're getting a replacement sorted for you, I'll have someone down there as soon as I can. In the meantime, the big blue and white machine is the one you want, Joe…' Richard Meyer's dry sense of humour lightened the tension a little.

'Good to know, thanks. The patient's stable and I think our best option is to continue. You're logged into my monitor?'

Bel hadn't even been aware that the anaesthetic machines were networked. But Joe seemed to know just as much about everyone else's jobs in Theatre as he did his own.

'Yes. Everything looks fine.'

'Good. Tim, is Sofia coming round?'

'No, but her breathing's okay and I've called for a gurney.' Sofia was lying on the floor in the recovery position and Tim had been monitoring her.

'Good. Make sure she's being seen by a doctor and then scrub back in. We'll be needing you.'

Joe quickly went through what everyone needed to do to cover for their missing colleagues, receiving acknowledgements from each member of the team.

'Right then. Let's show 'em what we're made of…'

He'd turned a potential crisis into a short pause for breath. Bel stepped forward, ready to start work again.

It took another three hours to knit a broken body back together again. When their patient was finally wheeled through into the recovery room there was a palpable sense of achievement.

'First time I've ever seen that happen,' the scrub nurse remarked. Student nurses and doctors fainted all the time in Theatre, but no one had heard of an anaesthesiologist passing out. 'Maybe Sofia's not well.'

'We'll see.' Joe had obviously been concerned for Sofia, but he didn't seem to want to pass an opinion. 'You all deserve a pat on the back for rallying round.'

'Any of that champagne left over from the weekend, Bel?' Amy chuckled and Bel saw Joe stiffen.

'Afraid not. It was a tough job drinking it, but somebody had to do it. Next time we'll be sure to invite you to give us a hand.' Bel saw Joe relax again. The sting of that newspaper article seemed like an inconsequential pinprick here, where life and death were the only things that really mattered.

'No, don't do that.' Amy shot her an expression of mock horror. 'I'd be telling operating theatre jokes.' She turned the corners of her mouth down, and everyone laughed.

'Interesting, though. I often wonder how people are going to get on after they leave here,' Tim mused.

'Well, drop in for coffee and find out. Everyone knows where we are now.' Bel grinned at Joe.

'Yes, we should,' Amy agreed. 'Did you raise the cash you needed?'

'Bel did a fine job. We'll be able to keep going for a while now, thanks to her.' The pride in Joe's voice sent tingles down her spine.

'Nice one. How's it feel to be rescued by the heroine of the hour then, Joe?' Amy teased him.

'How *does* it feel then? Being rescued?' Bel nudged Joe as they walked together out of the hospital.

'Better than I thought. Fewer bruises and I have no signs of altitude sickness. How does it feel to be the heroine of the hour?'

'That's better than I thought, too. Thanks for setting me straight.'

He chuckled. 'Any time. Although I think you set yourself straight, didn't you?'

It was difficult to tell. Maybe they'd just done it together, and the priorities of the operating theatre had finished the job. 'Did you get to speak to Sofia?'

He nodded. 'Yeah, she was feeling much better, but she was out for a while. They've arranged for some tests for epilepsy and she'll be seeing a specialist. I have to admit that was the first thing that occurred to me—it just didn't seem like a fainting fit.'

'They're obviously taking it seriously, then. But epilepsy isn't good news for someone working in an operating theatre.'

'We'll have to wait and see. I knew a nurse back in London whose epilepsy was controlled and she'd returned to work in Theatre after two years. Sofia's great with patients and she's a good doctor, and if the hospital needs to modify her role to support her they're obliged to do that.'

'You're always so committed to making things work for people, Joe. Helping them live their best lives.'

He put his arm around her shoulders, pulling her in close as they walked. 'You asked me once whether I thought we were living our best lives.'

A little thrill ran down her spine. 'And what do you reckon?'

'This is my best life. Right here, right now. I want to hold on to it.'

'I do too. We'll do it together, shall we?' It felt like a promise. One that Bel intended to keep.

CHAPTER ELEVEN

SO MUCH HAD happened in the last three months. Bel had come to Italy to reclaim the peace that she'd lost in London, and Rome had brought her so much more than she'd expected. The proud history and the vibrant streets were still as she remembered them from her childhood, and now she had the added pleasure of living and working here, in a job she loved. But the best thing about Rome had been Joe. The Englishman who'd grown up just a few miles away from her, but who she'd travelled more than a thousand miles to find.

The eve of her thirty-second birthday fell on a Friday, and Joe had taken the day off from the clinic. He'd booked lunch at a small restaurant in the Piazza Navona, and laid a wrapped parcel on the table when they sat down.

'Since you're going back to London for your birthday, I'd better give this to you now.'

Bel caught her breath. She knew that Joe must have dipped into the money he was putting aside each week for the deposit on a new apartment in order to afford the restaurant, but telling him that a present was far too much would dent his pride. She closed her eyes, letting her fingers explore the shape of the parcel.

'It's a book, isn't it.' And so carefully wrapped, the green marbled paper obviously handmade. 'I'm not going to open it yet. I just want to appreciate it for a while.' She wanted to make this moment last.

He chuckled, obviously pleased that she'd noticed the care he'd taken. Bel had never had to think about what she might spend her last penny on, and Joe's decision to spend his limited funds on a present for her said far more than anything he could possibly buy her.

'Okay. You think you can last out until coffee?'

Bel smiled back at him. 'I'm not sure… I'll have to now you've said it. I wish I wasn't going home now. That I could spend this weekend with you.'

He shook his head, frowning at the idea. 'We'll have plenty of weekends together. This one's special and you should spend it with your family. That's a gift you shouldn't refuse.'

He could so easily have persuaded her to stay here in Rome, but he'd been generous in that respect, too. Joe hadn't had enough family birthdays and it seemed important to him that Bel should have hers.

Lunch had been far too good to rush, angel-hair pasta with a delicious seafood sauce, followed by creamy panna cotta. But as soon as Joe signalled the waiter and ordered coffee, Bel picked up her present, carefully peeling the sticky tape back.

'Joe! It's beautiful—wherever did you get this?' The leather-bound copy of *The Moonstone* was showing its age a little. The gold lettering on the spine was slightly worn and when Bel opened it, the gilded edge of the pages had rubbed off in places. But that only showed that it had been read, which made it seem even more precious.

'I had to phone around a few second-hand booksellers in London to find a copy in decent condition. Look at the inside of the front cover…' His mouth turned down in a sudden expression of nerves about the gift.

Bel flipped back to the front of the volume, and caught her breath. Its first owner had written their name in the top left-hand corner, along with the date. The second had followed suit and then the third… Halfway down there were three names bearing the same surname, where the book had obviously been passed from one member of a family to another.

'Joe! This is wonderful. All of the people who've looked after this book and read it before me.' Bel read through the names, which spanned almost a hundred years. The first were written in copperplate script using a fountain pen, and later ones in more modern handwriting styles with a ballpoint.

He was grinning now, and proffering a pen. Bel took it gingerly. 'Perhaps I need to practise first.'

'Just write your name. Your own handwriting's good enough—that's what everyone else has done.'

The waiter brought the coffee and Bel snatched the book up, hugging it to her chest, well out of the way of any potential spills. Joe chuckled, moving both cups across the table towards him, and Bel cleared a space on the table in front of her. He seemed to be enjoying this impromptu ritual as much as she was, and he watched her carefully as she wrote.

Isabella Trueman. Bel decided that she should be the first to institute a new trend and wrote *Rome*, before adding the date. The moment was caught now, preserved, like all the other moments when this book had gained a new owner.

'You want to read the first few pages over coffee?' he asked and Bel shook her head.

'We have to read it together, don't we?'

'Not necessarily. I can read one book, you

read another. I've never had a three-book romance before.' He seemed to like the idea of breaking his own record.

'Well, I'm not going to rush it. So if you want to get to four you'll just have to stay around for a while longer.' The silent, implicit promise was enough and she'd savour each page.

They'd spent a few hours in the piazza, the small shops and street performers quite enough to hold their attention for a while. Then they'd fetched her suitcase from her apartment and boarded the train for the airport. Joe stopped at the departure gate, kissing her.

'I'll give your regards to London.' Bel smiled up at him.

He shrugged. Joe had moved on from London, and its treasures seemed to mean nothing to him. 'You can if you want.' He bent to kiss her again. '*Arrivederci*, Isabella.'

They didn't speak Italian when they were alone together, and somehow the words meant something. Joe had made a home here in Rome. A home that included her. Ten books, twenty or thirty even, suddenly seemed well within their grasp.

'*Arrivederci*, Joe...' She'd see him again soon.

The weekend had been wonderful. Her parents had both remarked on how well she was looking, and Bel had privately given Joe the credit for that. She wouldn't have any trouble in persuading them to come and visit her in Rome, and when they did they'd know that she'd finally made the right decision when it came to choice of partner. There was no rush and she'd take that at whatever pace Joe felt comfortable with.

They'd heard all about the clinic from Uncle Edo, although he'd kept his promise and not mentioned that Joe was more to her than just its founder and director. Her father had questioned her closely about how it was run over after-dinner brandy on Friday evening, but her mother had silenced him on Saturday morning, waving her finger at him and declaring that today there was no time for business. There were presents—a silk shirt from her mother and a new travelling bag from her father—and a party in the evening, under the sparkling lights of the large patio at the back of the house. Sunday was for sleeping in, and then taking Wilf for a long walk with her father, while her mother prepared a late lunch.

And then... Monday. Bel was flying back to Rome in the evening, and as soon as they'd finished breakfast her father had beckoned her into his study and waved her towards one of the leather-bound seats that stood around the fireplace.

'What's this, Dad?' The large, airy study was

for business only, and her mother usually only ever crossed the threshold to haul him out of it, telling him he'd spent long enough in here and there were other things to do.

'There's something I want to discuss with you.' Her father batted away Bel's questions about his health, telling her that his heart was functioning perfectly well and that he intended keeping it that way. 'This is about *you*, Bel. And the trust I established for you when you went to medical school.'

'That was a long time ago.' Bel had forgotten all about the small trust that her father had set up, which was intended to give her enough to make a start when she began work.

'Yes. You told me that you had a lot more studying to do after you qualified as a doctor and you didn't need it yet. And then…' Her father waved his hand.

'Then I met Rory. And things went a bit pear-shaped for a while.' When Bel had first met Rory she'd thought her only future was with him. And after that she hadn't been able to contemplate a future of any kind, she'd been too bound up in trying to clear herself of the charges levelled against her.

Her father smiled. 'So you're saying his name now, are you?'

Since she'd been with Joe, *his* was the only

name that made her feel anything. 'I've been leaving all of that behind me, Dad. You said I'd eventually get to that point and it turns out that you were right.'

'Then this *is* the right time.' Her father smiled, walking over to his desk to fetch a document holder, which he handed to her. 'I intended to give this to you on your thirtieth birthday, but we were all making decisions about how to get from one day to the next and it would have just been another thing you had to think about.'

Bel nodded. That birthday had been one she'd rather forget, coming right in the middle of the enquiry into her own part in Rory's fraudulent dealings. 'You were right. I was already panicking about you paying for the legal help I needed, because I didn't want to look like some rich kid who was above the rules. I think that anything else would have sent me right over the edge.'

'I know. But the trust is still there and I've been adding to it a bit over the years. In response to various changes.'

Bel shot him a reproachful look and he shrugged.

'You're my only child, Isabella. What else am I supposed to do with it?'

'You and Mum have always been so sure about me making my own way in life. And you were right, I really appreciate the chance you gave me to do so.'

'Move with the times, darling. You've carved out a place for yourself and you're someone who can do a lot of good in the world—someone who *wants* to do a lot of good in the world. Your mother and I are very proud of you and this is something to help you on your way with that.'

Bel opened the file and took out the typed balance sheet which lay on top of the papers and documents inside. There had been regular additions over the years, including a large one at about the time she'd told her parents she wanted to get married, and another when it had looked as if the charges against her could become a criminal matter, which might result in her name being removed from the medical register. A third, very substantial, sum had been added a few weeks ago, presumably after Uncle Edo had reported back on the work being done at the clinic. This was the kind of money that her father usually dealt in, and which her parents had always protected her from.

'Dad! What on earth were you thinking? This isn't just something to help me on my way...'

A three-book affair. Joe's relationships usually only ran to a few Sunday newspapers, if he was lucky. Three books had always been way beyond his comfort zone.

And yet somehow, this time it wasn't. When Bel returned from London the bookmark between the pages of *The Moonstone* showed that she'd already made a start. And by the time they'd reached the weekend she was a third of the way through, and Joe was contemplating whether another book might be an appropriate gift, or if he should leave it to Bel to choose her own reading matter.

'I've got something to discuss with you.' They'd got up late on Sunday morning and Bel was making breakfast. Joe had turned his hand to sandwiches for later, to sustain them on their ongoing exploration of the Via Appia.

'Yeah?' He looked up at her. Bel was particularly beautiful this morning, and he guessed that he might be under the influence of having missed her last weekend, and over the course of a busy week. Allowing himself to miss someone was new, too. 'Shall we do it in the open air, while we walk?'

She nodded, her brow puckering in an uncertain frown. Maybe it was more urgent than that. He turned, reaching out to caress her cheek.

'It won't wait that long? Is something bothering you?'

'It'll wait.' Bel seemed to come to a decision.

'It's nothing bad, and talking as we walk is a much better idea.'

The day began to move forward again. A slow, relaxed progress that made breakfast something to be savoured and the bus ride to the Via Appia time well spent. They took a short cut to the point on the road they'd reached the last time, and resumed their slow pace along the cobbles. His rucksack was a little lighter this time, since it contained only their lunch. Bel had thrown his clothes from yesterday into the washing machine this morning, and he'd left them behind to finish drying with hers. One more step along a road that Joe had never thought he would take.

'What's this thing that you want to discuss, then?' He turned his face up to a clear sky, feeling the warmth of the sun on his skin.

'My father dropped a bit of a bombshell on me when I went home. Apparently, I have a trust fund…'

'Yeah? I thought that was against his rules.'

Bel's laugh in response sounded a little nervous. 'He set it up when I first went to medical school. It was a few thousand, just to help me on my way when I needed it. I knew he'd done it, but I'd forgotten all about it. Apparently, he hasn't and he's been adding to it.'

A few thousand sounded like admirable restraint. Even if that now ran to a few hundred thousand, Joe couldn't imagine that it would be enough to change Bel's life. She was just reacting to the idea of a trust fund, but she should look at it as an opportunity to take on new challenges, as and when they presented themselves. The idea left him surprisingly unconcerned.

'We've been through this before, Bel. I know you've been hurt by the way that others have seen your father's wealth, but this is a good thing, isn't it? That you feel ready to accept whatever he's set aside for you.'

She smiled. 'I hoped you might see it that way. And yes, it's a very good thing. He'd planned on making the trust available to me when I was thirty but at that point we were still working through all of the problems with my ex. We've both managed to leave that behind now.'

'I'm glad to hear it. And you don't need to gain my approval, or even mention it to me. It's not my business, and I'm over the shock of finding myself in a relationship with someone whose father could buy her a whole hospital for Christmas if he wanted.'

'That's… Don't joke about it, Joe.'

There was something very confronting about the way that Bel seemed to be taking a stupid joke so literally. 'I didn't mean an actual hospital.'

'No, it's not quite as much as that. But he's

given me enough that… I can either do nothing for the rest of my life, or I can do something significant. Something that makes a real difference.'

'And which do you plan to go for?' Joe reckoned he knew the answer to that question. Her father probably did as well, and that was why he'd chosen this particular time to tell Bel about the trust.

She rolled her eyes. 'You mean die of boredom, or do what I've always wanted to do? Take a guess, Joe.'

'Just checking. This is your father's understanding of the situation as well?'

'Yes, of course it is. You don't suppose he'd offer me cash if he thought I'd see that as an opportunity to throw away everything I've worked for, do you?'

'That's not the impression I have of him. Can we sit down for a minute?' Joe could feel changes coming, and he reminded himself that change wasn't always a bad thing. It wouldn't be a bad thing for Bel—it sounded as if she'd just been given a significant opportunity. That meant that whatever happened next mustn't be a bad thing for him.

They left the road, finding a secluded spot to sit on the grass. Bel produced several folded sheets of paper from her bag and handed them to him, telling Joe that she wanted him to read them through when he again mentioned it was really none of his business.

'This…it's not just money, is it. There's a whole investment and property portfolio here.'

Bel nodded. 'The idea is that whatever I decide to do is self-sustaining. There's cash to set up a project, and an income to keep it going. Or I could use another financial model. It's not all about medical choices, it's about commercial choices as well. I don't really understand all of the options right now. Dad said that he can help me.'

Something cold closed around Joe's heart. This was a once-in-a-lifetime opportunity. More than that, it was an opportunity that was only ever offered to the very rich. Bel had to take it.

'So you'll be going back to London?'

'For a little while. Not for good—nothing needs to change between us.'

Everything needed to change. For a woman who'd had every opportunity that life could offer her, Bel just wasn't thinking big enough. She'd realise that soon enough and that one city couldn't contain all of the possibilities that her father had just made available to her.

Joe had thought this equation through already. He'd left London because he couldn't deal with the memories of loss and the grief after his parents died. Rome had allowed him to function again, beyond the obvious necessities of work and sleep, and he'd set up the clinic knowing that it was his last chance. Poured everything he had into it, not just financially but emotionally.

He and Bel had reached for the 'best life' that they both wanted. But maybe Joe had been foolish to believe that it would be any different from the other promises he'd been made every time he'd gone to a new family. Maybe he should have trusted his experience a little better, and realised that Bel would ultimately leave, in just the same way that everyone else had.

If he followed her now, he'd sooner or later want to build something else of his own. And the next time her opportunities were too good to miss, his world would come crashing down again. No relationship could withstand that and it was better for both of them if he lost her now, rather than holding on and trying to believe that there could be any other ending for them. The thought was like a physical blow, leaving him almost stunned at its force.

Or—maybe it wasn't quite as straightforward as that. Bel wouldn't just leave him behind, so he'd have to find a way to make her go. That thought hurt even more, although, of all people, Joe should know how to deal with the loss of having to move on.

A sudden quiet settled on him. He knew what happened next, he'd done it enough times before. He'd keep the part of him that he could truly call his own sheltered from the storms of having to say goodbye. Joe would walk away, so numb that he could hardly feel anything.

CHAPTER TWELVE

BEL HAD CHOSEN her moment to tell Joe about the trust, and maybe that had been wise. He seemed to be taking all of this surprisingly well. There was no reason why the clinic couldn't benefit from the trust. He might draw the line at that, but Bel reckoned that they could come to an agreement that would work for everyone. And he seemed to be totally on board with the idea that she'd be in control of a very large amount of money.

'It'll work, Joe. It's a lot of money and I'd have to give up my job at the hospital. But I can put myself on a similar salary to what I earn there, so in practice nothing much is going to change. I just get to work on something that…' She wanted it to be something that she and Joe could build together, more than anything. Her dad might urge caution in that respect, for obvious reasons, but he could build in as many safeguards as he liked because she trusted Joe. She needed his strength and expertise to help her.

'*We* could work on something that matters. I wouldn't for one moment ask you to give up the clinic, but between us we could do a lot more than I can do alone.'

He shook his head. 'It's a nice thought, and thank you for trusting me with it. How long have we known each other?'

'If that's the way you feel…' Bel thought for a moment. 'We could know each other for a while longer. None of these decisions need to be made straight away.'

'You do need to make some decisions. And they're too important to make if you're starting out with conditions. Like having to be in any one particular place.'

He was so cool. Almost cold. And frighteningly assured.

'Joe, this isn't a way for my dad to get me back to London. Mum and Dad would obviously like that, but I'm thirty-two years old. I'm allowed to work wherever I want to work, it's not as if they don't have the capacity to visit as often as they like.'

'I know. But I can't—I won't—tie you down.'

Suddenly Bel knew as well. He'd already said goodbye to her. Joe had closed down, the same way he'd learned to close down every time that he lost something. Some*one*. He wouldn't talk about her and he'd do his best not to think about her.

'Can't we talk about it? You could stay here and find someone to run the clinic. Join me when you can?' That was a last-ditch attempt to save their relationship, and Bel knew that Joe could never agree to it.

'The clinic is what I have, Bel. I've built it from nothing and… It may not be much in comparison with what you're able to build now. But it's my achievement, the thing I feel most proud of.'

She'd been so wrong to trust him. Rory had acted out of greed and self-interest, and Joe… His motives were very different, his painful childhood had taught him lessons that he couldn't forget now. And he wanted her to leave and take the opportunities that he'd never had. Maybe she should respect him for that, but she couldn't because it all boiled down to one thing. Her trust in Rory had been misplaced and her trust in Joe had, too.

'I see that. I should never have asked you to give the clinic up, I know how much it means to you.' Still, she couldn't walk away from him. If she kept a dialogue going then there was a chance that they might find a way through this. 'Can we go back now? I don't want to walk any more.'

'Of course.' He got to his feet, holding out his hand to help her up. Bel took it automatically, and wished she hadn't. The touch of his fingers was almost too much to bear.

They walked back to the bus stop in silence, and thankfully there was only a five-minute wait. She wanted to scream, throw something at him. Anything, to break through the reserve that protected his heart from pain. Somehow, she managed to find something to say, pointing out things along the way, and Joe replied every time. It was torment by polite conversation, but it was better than nothing at all.

Her heart started to beat a little faster as he followed her up to her apartment. Perhaps she was wrong. Maybe he was still here and he'd save her after all. They'd argue, shout a little, perhaps even break a little china in the process, but they'd work something out. Then Joe dashed all of her hopes.

'If it's going to be awkward at work, I can speak to HR and swap to the night shift for a while.'

Bel shook her head. 'No, it's okay. I'm nearly at the end of my three-month probationary period and the hospital's due to send me a new contract but they haven't yet, so I'm well within my rights to leave immediately. You know there's a waiting list for doctors who want to transfer to the trauma department?'

Joe's look of surprise was an agonising reminder that he still had some emotion left. Just none for her any more. 'I didn't, actually.'

'They told me that when I joined. They won't have any trouble in getting a replacement for me.'

'Someone to do your job. Not a replacement.' His face softened fleetingly, but then he was back to the practicalities. 'I'll just take my clothes, then…'

'You could leave them here. I won't be going anywhere for a few weeks, there are things to be sorted out.' That was about as close as Bel could get to begging, when she was just as angry as she was heartbroken.

He hesitated but shook his head. 'We said that we couldn't make each other any promises, when we started out. I hope that you can understand why I won't be back, and that we can part as friends.'

Friends? They'd been doctors, lovers, people who aired their differences by quarrelling loudly and often… Anything that involved a bit of passion. She and Joe had never been just friends. But it seemed that was all they were left with.

'Of course.'

He nodded stiffly. 'Thank you. I appreciate it.'

Joe hurried to collect his things, stuffing them into his backpack as he made for the front door. Bel didn't move. She wasn't going to help him go by opening and then closing the door. He'd have to do that all by himself.

But he didn't look back. When Bel ran to the window she saw him walking away quickly, his gait purposeful.

She was done with him. Joe had let her down, just when she needed him the most, and she couldn't forgive him for that. It would hurt for a while and then she'd be free of him, just as she was free of Rory. The only problem with that was that she knew in her heart that she could never stop loving Joe.

Moving on was a great deal more difficult than it had been when he was a child. Then he hadn't had to actually do anything, he'd just followed the instructions of the adults around him. Joe had been able to allow numbness to carry him through the transition between one set of welcoming faces and another, and concentrated on finding out whether he'd be allowed to take a book from a new set of shelves and read it. Now it was more as if his whole body was shutting down. He couldn't breathe, and his heart felt as if it had been torn from his chest.

He kept walking. Straight past his apartment, because although Bel hadn't spent a great deal of time there, his main attachment to it was that it did hold some memories of her. Past the hospital, because he didn't want to contemplate the thought that she'd have to turn up there at some point, to tell them that she wouldn't be signing a new contract. The places they'd been together were no-go areas for the time being, but maybe that would change.

He had to go somewhere. Leaving might be the same, something that ran through his life like an unbreakable thread, but when he was a kid there had always been a new place to go, with food on the table and a bed to sleep in. This time he had to fend for himself.

Joe stopped at a café, ordering pizza slices and hot chocolate. Now that his stomach was full, he needed to find a bed for the night. He started to walk again, and found himself outside the clinic. Here, there were other memories, which might soften the shock of losing Bel.

He climbed the stairs to his office and stared at the blank screen of his laptop for an hour. Then he went downstairs and polished Maria's desk, reckoning that if nothing else could come of the evening, at least she might notice and be pleased with the gesture. He cleaned the kitchen and looked for any minor specks of dust in the consulting rooms which might claim his attention for a few minutes, then fell asleep on the sofa in the reception area. Waking early, with the impression of sound and colour still in his mind from dreams he couldn't remember, he made his way to work.

Bel had spent a week locked in her apartment, going out only when she needed to buy food. She'd cried a lot and raged at Joe, but still she'd waited for his call. When it didn't come, she'd called her father, asking when they could start work on plans for the trust, knowing that 'now' was always his preferred option. She'd packed her bags at the weekend and flown back to London, ready to start work on Monday morning.

One thing about her parents' house in Chelsea was that she had no opportunity to dwell on her feelings. There were papers to read and discussions with lawyers and accountants to fill her time. She'd never realised that the process of working out how to spend money could be so complicated.

The Moonstone lay on her bedside table, reminding her that she and Joe had only ever managed to finish one book together. She'd abandoned this story, although she couldn't put the book away on a shelf. It was a reminder. That she'd loved Joe, and even if he'd let her go, they'd had something real.

But the stress of hidden emotion was exhausting. She'd spent Sunday morning in her pyjamas, unable to sleep but not ready to get dressed and go downstairs yet.

'Not feeling well?' Her father appeared in her bedroom doorway.

'I'm fine, Dad. Just a bit tired, this last week's been a bit full-on.'

He nodded. 'Well, you need to get up now. We have a meeting.'

'On Sunday? What about lunch?' Sunday lunch was sacrosanct, and Dad would be catching the sharp side of Mum's tongue if he broke that particular rule.

'It was your mother's idea. Get dressed, we're going in thirty minutes.'

'Where?'

'The Hidden Door.' Her father smiled. 'It's important.'

It must be. The Hidden Door was probably the most exclusive restaurant in London, situated behind a popular Chelsea eatery, where people went to see and be seen. In contrast, The Hidden Door was where you went if you wanted to eat out in the knowledge that you wouldn't be seen, and its hand-picked clientele was selected from the ranks of the very rich and the very famous.

'What am I wearing, Dad?' Bel called after her father.

'Clothes, I imagine. Not my territory...ask your mother...'

She heard his voice from the other end of the hallway, and then Wilf's excited yelp as he whistled to him to come and play catch in the garden while Bel showered and dressed.

Her father was waiting in the car exactly thirty minutes later, and Bel's mother shooed her out of the front door. There wasn't a great deal of time to wonder what all the rush was about or who they'd be meeting, and ten minutes later they drew into an undercover driveway behind the main restaurant. A parking valet collected the car keys and opened what looked like a service doorway, which led to a small foyer.

'Mr Trueman. How nice to see you. We have table four ready for you.' The concierge guided them into the dining room, where six tables were carefully arranged to afford space and privacy to each party of diners. A waiter pulled out a chair for Bel and she sat down.

'This table's set for two. Who are we meeting?'

'I'm meeting with you.' Her father dismissed the waiter with a twitch of his finger. 'Or I suppose we could say that you're meeting with me.'

'Couldn't we have done that at home? In the kitchen?'

'I don't have as good a selection of wine. And

I haven't been here for ages, I hear they have a new menu.'

'Dad, you're not steamrollering some business contact of yours into submission, this is me you're talking to. Why did you haul me out of bed and bring me all the way down here?'

Her father nodded. 'Because the outcome of the conversation we're about to have may affect your trust. And you're my daughter and I wanted to treat you to a nice lunch.'

'Okay. Better. Are we going to have a glass of wine, then? You choose it...'

Her father beckoned to their waiter, ignoring the wine list and ordering a whole bottle of one of his favourite vintages. Things were obviously getting serious.

'I'm going to put my cards on the table, Isabella. Your mother heard a noise and found you crying in your sleep earlier this week. She sat with you and sang a lullaby and you quietened down a bit. Do you remember that?'

Bel shook her head, feeling herself flush with embarrassment. 'No, I... It must have been a dream, Dad. I'm sorry, I know that would have worried her and I wish that hadn't happened. Let's go, I'll explain everything to her.'

Her father laid his hand on hers. 'You mean you'll come out with a whole string of excuses and try to convince her that everything's all right? That's not going to wash, I'm afraid, because the things that worry a parent the most are those that their child won't tell them about. She called Edoardo the next day, and it took her ten minutes to break him down. He said that it was rare to see a couple so made for each other.'

'When I accepted the donation for the clinic from you…there was nothing going on between me and Joe then.' Bel pressed her lips together miserably.

'I appreciate you telling me that, but it wouldn't have mattered if there was. The money I sent to the clinic was an investment in people's futures, and the updates and photographs I've received have given me a great deal of pleasure. He seems to be a good man.'

'He is, Dad. A really good man…' The waiter approached with the wine, and her father took the bottle from him before he could begin with the ritual of displaying the label and pouring a mouthful for him to taste.

'Thank you, Sam, that's splendid. May we have a few minutes, please?'

'Of course, Mr Trueman. Call me when you're ready to order.'

Her father turned his gaze back onto Bel as he poured the wine. 'Why don't you tell me all about it, Isabella? Maybe I can help and maybe not. But I *can* listen.'

* * *

It had all come tumbling out. The way that the clinic was helping people in ways that Bel hadn't even thought about before. How much she'd learned, and how committed Joe was to his patients. Her father listened quietly, stopping her only to order a mixed plate of starters.

'But you haven't included the clinic in your plans for the future.' Dad was being tactful. What he really meant was that Joe wasn't included in her plans.

'It's complicated.'

'Of course it is. When is it not?' Her father leaned back in his seat. 'But it sounds to me as if you love him. Is that the word you're afraid to say?'

She couldn't even say it now. Even though it was the only thing that made any sense to Bel. 'Dad… Can the trust wait?'

'Of course. It'll be there whenever you want it, that was always my intention. You don't owe it your attention if you have other things to do.'

A weight seemed to lift from her shoulders. 'I think I do have other things right now.'

Her father nodded. He was always at his most focused when there was something to be done. 'In that case, I recommend a square meal for starters. You've hardly been eating this last week. Shall I order…?'

* * *

Joe had lost track of the days, because suddenly the nights had become so much more important. That was when he could bring Bel back to him, even though the memories always involved a sense of heartbreaking loss.

He'd kept going, though, because that was all he knew how to do. On Friday, Maria brought him to a screeching halt.

'Where's Bel? She's not sick, is she?'

For all Joe knew, she might be. She could be here still, in Italy, or she could already have flown back to London. That was one of the hardest parts. He'd always known more or less where Bel was, and when he might see her again. But now he was adrift. Becalmed on a lonely sea, without any idea which way he should go to reach his next destination.

'She's going back to London. There was… an opportunity there for her that she couldn't miss.' *That* was better. He'd acknowledged for the first time that Bel was gone, and maybe now he could move on.

'An *opportunity*? And so she just dropped everything and left?' Maria was bristling with disapproval now.

'It was…' He couldn't allow Maria to think that Bel was at fault. 'There really wasn't any choice about it. I told her that, and that she should go.'

'Joe!' Maria frowned angrily at him.

'What? You think I should have lied to her? Asked her to stay when it was in her own best interests to go?' However much the truth had cost him, he'd had to face it.

'And what do you suppose a woman does when you ask her to stay?'

Joe shrugged. He'd never been in that position before.

'She makes up her own mind.' Maria supplied him with the answer. 'But when you tell her to go, you give her no choice. She goes.'

Joe hadn't thought of it in quite that way before. But he wasn't going to argue—it at least put the responsibility squarely onto his shoulders. 'I suppose so…'

Maria puffed out an exasperated breath. Clearly, she wasn't done with him yet. 'What are you doing on Sunday?'

That was a *very* sore point. He imagined that Maria probably knew that, and didn't care. 'I'll think of something.'

'Right, then. You're coming to lunch. Both my daughters are coming as well as my son and his family, but we'll make room. We can't have you moping.'

Joe wasn't aware he *had* been moping. Not in

public, at least. What he did in his own time was his business. 'Don't think I don't appreciate the invitation. I'm okay about it all though...'

'You want my son to have to come and fetch you?' That was an obvious threat, since Maria's son was an officer of the Polizia di Stato. 'He could arrest you if you don't show up.'

Joe held up his hands in surrender. 'Thanks, Maria. I'll look forward to it.'

Lunch had been a long and slightly riotous affair. Maria's husband, her son and his wife and her two daughters had all made him welcome, treating him as if he were a part of the family and expecting him to pile in and help with whatever needed to be done to get lunch on the two different tables that had been pushed together under a large sunshade in the garden.

But the one clear image in Joe's head as he took the bus back to his apartment was Maria's grandson. He was only six, but had solemnly shaken Joe's hand, along with the older men, when he'd been getting ready to leave. Then he'd stretched his arms up, demanding a hug.

'*Arrivederci*, Joe.' His words were the same as everyone else's. The same as the ones he'd exchanged with Bel at the airport, when he'd seen her off on her birthday weekend. He was just a child but he already knew how to say goodbye without turning it into loss.

The sun was going down, and that was one more ending. Tomorrow might just be a new beginning, though.

CHAPTER THIRTEEN

It had been three weeks now. Joe had missed Bel for every waking moment, but he'd been busy. He'd moved forward with a determination that had almost frightened him at times, and now he was almost done.

But his last move was made for him. As he opened up the clinic on a bright Friday morning, he heard a car draw up. He recognised it before he remembered whose it was, and then saw Costanza in the driving seat. She tumbled out, her face tight with stress.

'Dr Dixon…'

No one ever called him that unless they needed his help. 'Is everything all right, Costanza?'

'My boy, Nico. He's hurt himself and… I know this is not what you are here for, but can you help, please? The hospital is so busy…'

Particularly in the early morning, when urgent care centres all over the city would still be dealing with the fallout from the night before. It was an environment that would challenge anyone, but an autistic child would find the noise and the people unbearable.

'How is he hurt, Costanza?' If taking Nico to the hospital was the only option, then perhaps Joe could accompany them, and ease their way a little.

'He fell and cut himself. Bel says that it will need to be cleaned and perhaps a couple of stitches…'

Bel. She was still here? Joe dismissed the thought. He knew that Bel wouldn't have stayed in Rome for another three weeks when there was something for her to be doing in London. Maybe Costanza had phoned her.

Now wasn't the time to wonder about that. 'Bring him in, Costanza. No one else will be here for another couple of hours and we'll find somewhere he's happy with and take things at his pace.'

'Thank you. Thank you so much…' Costanza turned, beckoning towards the back seat of the car. And suddenly, it was as if a meteor had just appeared in the sky and was heading straight for him. Joe froze as the car door opened and Bel got out, her face twisted with the same agony that he felt.

'I'm so sorry, Joe. I didn't want…' She turned, and Joe saw little Nico behind her. He was pulling at his T-shirt and wore a pair of headphones to distract him from the early-morning activity of the city, but he allowed Bel to lay her hand on his shoulder, guiding him out of the car. His arm was bandaged in an obvious attempt to stop the bleeding, but Bel wouldn't have had what was needed to clean and stitch the wound at home and her decision to come here first, before trying the hospital, was the right one.

He had to breathe. Focus on the child. 'It's okay. Bring him in.' He stood back from the door, letting Costanza and Bel shepherd Nico inside.

They took their time. Bel had suggested that Nico might feel more at ease in the garden and Costanza had agreed. The boy had chosen a shaded corner, and Bel had fetched a seat for him, with one for Costanza and another for Joe. Blood was beginning to seep through the bandage, and Joe hurried to fetch the things he'd need from the clinic's first aid cupboard, arranging them on a tray.

'Joe…' He turned to see Bel standing behind him, once more in an agony of embarrassment.

'It's okay.' It really wasn't but it was all he could think of to say. 'Nico first.'

She nodded. 'Maybe we can talk?'

Joe wasn't sure if he was ready to talk just yet. But that could wait as well. 'Wash your hands, I'll be needing your help…'

When Bel followed him back to the garden the effortless synchronicity kicked in, almost knocking him sideways. Muscle memory, maybe. An echo of the concentrated focus of the operating theatre. Or maybe something more. But there were no words needed, they each knew exactly what to do, and the gash on Nico's arm was cleaned and stitched with the minimum of fuss.

'Well done, Nico.' The boy looked up at him and gave him a nod. 'Your arm will heal very well.'

'Will you look at it again?'

'Yes, I'll come to your home in one week and look at it.' Bel had been explaining what was going on to Nico every step of the way, but maybe she wouldn't be around to monitor the wound.

'Okay. That's all right.'

Joe smiled. Once they'd settled him and he'd begun to feel safe, Nico had been a much better patient than some adults, uncomplaining and co-operative.

'Thank you, Nico. It was very nice to meet you.'

Costanza was smiling now. 'Thank you so much. We so appreciate your time. What will this cost?'

'This is a free clinic.'

'But I can pay…' Costanza reached for her

handbag, clearly determined to give Joe something, but Bel laid her hand on her friend's arm.

'Perhaps you and Nico can make some biscuits and bring them here. Would you like that, Nico?'

Nico nodded and got to his feet, clearly ready to go home and make biscuits right now.

'Tomorrow, Nico. We'll make biscuits tomorrow.' Costanza gathered up their things and shook Joe's hand warmly. 'Thank you again, Joe.'

'My pleasure…'

Suddenly the haze of uncertainty descended on him again. And then Joe remembered what Maria had told him. Essentially, if you ask a woman to stay, she'll make up her own mind.

He turned to Bel, his heart lurching in a mixture of terror and joy. Now was the time, and he had to grasp it. She was fidgeting uncertainly, but that only increased his resolve.

'Please stay.'

She nodded, and sat down in the seat he'd been occupying. Bel said her goodbyes to Nico and Costanza, and left Joe to accompany them through to the front door. He waited for them to get settled in the car, and waved as they drove away.

Suddenly he couldn't breathe. He had no idea why Bel was back here in Rome. He wasn't ready yet…

Too bad. Bel was here and that was all that mattered. If he had to go into this situation unprepared, then so be it.

Bel hadn't wanted to just turn up on Joe's doorstep again. He'd retreated from her, doggedly and uncomplainingly, and ever since she'd flown back to Italy three days ago she'd been pondering the best way to approach him. Then Costanza had banged on the door of her apartment, holding Nico in her arms. One look at the blood dripping from the gash on his arm had told her that the boy needed more than just a plaster, and Bel hadn't been able to think of a better place to bring him.

Joe had been here, as he always was, and he'd been so good with Nico. Talking *to* him, rather than straight over his head, making sure that he understood what was going on. Nico had responded to that, and so had Costanza. And there was still something there between her and Joe. So strong that it made her heart break all over again, into too many pieces to just pick them all up and leave.

When he came back out into the garden his face was unreadable. But Joe was still there, she could see it in his eyes. He hadn't retreated behind the wall of polite rejection that had sent her away from here and back to London. That was something, at least. Maybe everything.

She got to her feet. 'Joe, I… I went to London. I'm back now. This isn't the right time for me to start thinking about what to do with the trust. I'm staying here, in Rome.'

Genuine surprise showed on his face. And something of the warmth that she so badly wanted from him. 'What does your father think about that?'

'He agrees with me. The trust was only ever meant to facilitate things that I wanted to do, not to take my life over. It'll wait.'

'Okay.' Joe was clearly trying to choose his words carefully. 'You're coming back to the hospital? The clinic?'

'No. My job at the hospital is probably filled, and I don't care about the clinic…' That wasn't true. 'I mean that's not what I came back for. I came back for *you*, Joe. I know you told me to leave, but you were wrong. And I was wrong to listen to you, so I'm going to correct that error of judgement.' She folded her arms defiantly. That probably wasn't the best way to tell him what she'd been meaning to say, but it was a relief to just say it, without beating about the bush.

He smiled suddenly. 'Someone told me that if you tell a woman to leave—'

'Forget whatever anyone's told you, Joe. Listen to me. Now.'

His lip curled. The thrill of battle ignited in

his eyes. That gave her courage, because she was here to finally fight for what she wanted. 'All right, let's talk about now. You turn your back on the opportunity of a lifetime and show up here. No job. Do you even have a place to live?'

'My apartment's on a six-month lease. And what was I going to do, tell Costanza to deal with Nico on her own?'

'That's *not* what I meant, Isabella. Of course you should have brought Nico here. But you have a family and opportunities. Don't ever think that doesn't matter in life.'

He needed to hear this in words of one syllable. That was okay, Bel could do that. 'I know how much you've lost, Joe. And I know that the only home and opportunities you have are the ones you've made for yourself. But I need you to understand that my family and my opportunities will always wait for me. Right now, I need to be here and tell you that I love you.'

She'd finally said it. Moved past her fear of betrayal and trusted him. It felt like a release, even though she didn't dare hope that Joe could tell her that he loved her. Bel knew that he did, but it would take work before he was able to say it.

He reached forward, taking her hand. 'Come upstairs.'

'Where?'

'Just come upstairs. Please, Isabella.'

She never had been able to resist those blue eyes of his. Particularly when they were full of warmth and gazing at her. And he'd called her *Isabella*. That must mean something, even if it was all that Joe could do to articulate his feelings. Bel followed him up to the reception area, and then up the flight of stairs to the first floor. He walked through the largest of the consulting rooms, opening a door that Bel had always imagined led to a cupboard.

He was halfway up the narrow steps when she realised where they were going. 'Why are you bringing me up to the attic?'

'Nice view.' He turned, smiling as Bel rolled her eyes. Nothing had been talked about or settled, but the chemistry between them was there still. Bubbling and fizzing through her veins, telling her that everything was going to be all right if she just hung in there.

He opened a door at the top of the stairs and they stepped into a long, low space filled with boxes and dust, and partitioned off at one end. He'd told her that there was a living space up here, which wasn't used. Bel picked her way past the crates, and Joe led her through the door in the partition.

It was clean and bright, but that was about all you could say for it. Boxes were stacked in one corner and there was a sofa and a table. An arch led through to a small kitchen and there was another door, which probably led to a bathroom.

'Are you living here, Joe?'

'I moved in last week.' Joe looked around. 'It's not much at the moment, but it could be nice. I could knock a few holes in the partition and build another one further down if I need more room.'

'What happened with your apartment?'

'I gave it up. Now that we know we can keep the clinic running for more than just a month at a time, it became a possibility.'

Bel nodded. Joe could never have taken the risk of losing his home and why should he? He'd already ploughed most of the rest of his salary into the clinic. She walked over to the double doors at one end of the space, opening them. The back of the clinic faced the old part of the city, and the view really was spectacular, with terracotta roofs and ornate domes stretching out into the morning mist.

'And are you spending every waking moment working?' That had always been a reason for him not to move in here.

'No. I've been spending time on a lot of different things. Missing you…'

'Then this place could be really good for you, Joe. It'll give you a chance to get back on your feet financially.' At least he'd missed her, although he seemed to have forgotten what she'd said downstairs. That she loved him. It was okay. Maybe Joe needed a bit of time to process, and as long as he didn't send her away, she'd tell him every day until he believed her.

She heard his footsteps, moving across the room towards her. When she turned, he seemed very close. 'Isabella, I didn't ask you up here to talk about that. I wanted to make it clear to you that what you see right now is all I have.' He fell to one knee.

'Joe...' She tugged at his shoulder, but he wouldn't move.

'I love you, Isabella. I have nothing to offer you, other than that.'

'You have everything to offer me, Joe. All of the things I really need.' She bent, trying to get him back onto his feet again, but Joe was too solid. He wound his arm around her waist, and she sank down onto his knee.

'I didn't just let you go. I drove you away.' He hushed her when she started to disagree. 'I know what I did. I couldn't bear to lose you and so I just switched off, the way I've always done when I feel I'm losing something. I promise that I'll never do that again, because I intend to fight for you.'

She could feel tears on her cheeks. Bel wiped them away. 'That's good to hear. Because I intend to fight for you, too.' Maybe he'd kiss her now. She was aching to feel his kiss on her lips…

He smiled. 'Will you marry me?'

'Yes!' She flung her arms around his neck, holding him tight. 'When?'

He chuckled. 'As soon as we have a place to live and I can afford a nice ring for you. In the meantime…' Joe reached for the neck of his shirt, pulling at a piece of synthetic surgical thread which was threaded through a ring. There was no stone, but the gold love knot was just perfect on its own. Simple and solid, yet beautiful.

'It's gorgeous, Joe. I don't want another ring. I want this one.' She held out her hand so that he could slip the ring onto her finger. He pulled at the thread, but it didn't give. He slipped the ring onto her finger anyway.

'You'll have to strangle me to get away now.' He chuckled and Bel kissed him.

'I'm not going anywhere, Joe. Neither are you.'

'I can promise you that.' He kissed her, effortlessly capturing her in that familiar world where the only thing that mattered was that he was holding her, safe and warm in his arms.

'Did you hear the front door?' She kissed him again. There was no need to stop.

'Yeah.' Joe kissed her back.

'Perhaps we should...' One last kiss. Bel couldn't resist that.

'In a minute...'

They couldn't get enough of each other. Couldn't turn away from the happiness that enveloped them both. But Bel could hear footsteps on the stairs and then a voice.

'Joe! Are you up? Someone's opened the shutters downstairs.'

'That was me, Maria,' he called back. 'I'll be down in ten minutes...'

Bel heard Maria's footsteps go back down the stairs. 'Maybe eleven?'

'Twelve would be better.' He kissed her as if they had all the time in the world. 'I have patients this morning. Will you be at your apartment? I can be there at around lunchtime.'

'No, I'll be here. I'm sure I can make myself useful.'

'If you're off the premises I won't be tempted to come looking for you...'

'I told you that I wasn't going anywhere, Joe. This is who we are. We work hard and then we play well. I'm not going to be the kind of fiancée who hangs around waiting for you. You'd better get used to that.'

He grinned. 'I can get used to it. I didn't expect anything different...' Bel went to stand and he closed his fingers around her arm. 'Wait… Wait a moment. Take the ring off…'

'No! Get a pair of scissors if you can't break the thread. How long have you had it around your neck?'

'Ever since I bought it, four days ago. I was planning on coming to London as soon as I got paid in two weeks' time, but I knew what I wanted and I got some cash back on the deposit from my old apartment. The ring was a reminder that I wasn't going to give up on you, however long it took to prove myself.'

'You don't have to prove yourself to me, Joe. I know who you are, and I love you.'

'I love you, too.' His kiss left her in no doubt about that.

But it was time to go. He led her through into the kitchen, finding a pair of scissors and snipping the thread around his neck, his mouth quirking in a mock grimace. 'You can step away now. If you want to.'

'I'm never going to do that, Joe. Let's go downstairs and get on with the rest of our lives, shall we?'

CHAPTER FOURTEEN

Eighteen months later

A LOT HAD happened in the last eighteen months. But it had happened to them both together.

Joe had insisted she call her parents to share their news with them. Her mother had asked when they could visit, and Bel had relayed Joe's answer, telling them to come as soon as they liked. The next day, they'd been waiting for Bel and Joe in the hospital reception area, having already checked in to a nearby hotel.

Bel had wondered what her mother might say about the rooftop living space at the clinic, but clearly, she already liked Joe well enough to describe it as cosy and romantic, rather than cramped. Joe had taken them both on a tour of the clinic, and her father had nodded quietly, obviously much impressed by his work.

Bel had used the three months left on the lease of her apartment to clean and paint the attic and create a home for them up amongst the rooftops.

The hospital had taken her back, and she and Joe had continued their work there and at the clinic.

Their first visit to London had been tough. They'd taken a week off work and Bel had booked them into a hotel, because there were things they needed to do alone before going on to stay with her parents at the weekend. Joe had taken her to see the house he'd lived in with his parents, and then to the bank to unlock a safety deposit box that was full of photographs and mementos. It had been hard for him, but he'd sorted through everything, numb at first and then gripped by the grief he'd suppressed for so long. She'd held him as he wept, going through the pain of leaving the past behind to start a new life.

After a long evening spent with her father, bouncing ideas back and forth, they'd found ways of making the clinic self-supporting without compromising its core values. They'd worked, just as her father said they would, and now the clinic's future was assured on a permanent basis.

They'd worked hard during the week, but Sundays were still sacrosanct. Their time, to nourish their own relationship. And after a year it had been time to move on. They'd been so happy in their apartment amongst the rooftops of Rome, but there were new challenges and new places to beckon them on.

The clinic was expanding, into new and bigger premises. And Bel and Joe had found a villa that they loved, just outside Rome. They'd carefully packed the framed photographs of his parents, which Bel had added to over the months they'd been here. Her own photographs from when she was a child. Joe and her dad, laughing over something in a pavement café. A photo that her mum had taken of her and Joe, against the skyline of Rome. When Joe had expressed his regret over leaving their apartment, and promised that the first thing he'd do at the new house would be to find a place for their growing collection of family pictures, Bel had known that he was finally free.

They'd both needed to build a life together themselves, and her father had given in gracefully, offering them advice and support but letting them pay their own way. The wedding of Bel's dreams had been carefully put together with friends and family, and finally the November day had come.

'What's Dad doing with Joe?' Bel leaned out of her bedroom window, shivering in the cool breeze as she tried to see what was going on in the stone-built outhouse at the end of the garden, which was currently being converted into a home office.

'Advice on how to be a good husband, I expect.' Her mother was carefully removing a spot, which was invisible to the naked eye, from Bel's wedding shoes.

'How much advice does he need, Mum? Joe's got everything under control already.'

'I'm sure he'll think of something.' Her mother propelled her away from the window and closed it. 'He's taking his duties very seriously, you know.'

Both of her parents had. Since Joe had no family of his own, her father had diffidently wondered whether he might be considered as best man, leaving Bel's mother to give her away. Bel had loved the idea, and when she'd asked Joe he'd been touched that her father would do such a thing.

'Look! They're coming inside. He mustn't see you, darling.'

'I'm not wearing my dress yet, Mum. Joe's seen me in my pyjamas already this morning.'

Her mother frowned. 'But your hair… I've just brushed it out.'

'He's seen my hair before as well. It's okay, Mum, really. This is what I chose, an informal wedding. Let's just take a few breaths and relax, shall we?' Bel moved her hands up and then down again to indicate the tempo of slow, relaxing breaths, and her mother smiled.

'You're so serene, Isabella. Everything's just the way you want it.'

Bel hugged her mother. 'Yes, it is. And I can't

thank you and Dad enough, for going with the flow and letting us do things in our own way. It means so much to us both that you've supported us in that.'

'It's been our privilege, darling. I don't know quite how you turned out so level-headed, I expect it was your father's doing, but we couldn't be more proud of you. And Joe too, he's the son we were never able to have. I'm going to go downstairs and make some coffee, and Joe can bring yours up to you.'

'Thanks, Mum. Only may I have tea…?'

Five minutes later, Joe appeared in the doorway of their bedroom, grinning broadly. 'Your mum's in fine form. Very relaxed.'

'Just don't drop any of your coffee on my shoes…' Bel pushed the shoes out of sight, under the bed, as a concession to her mother.

'I can stay? There's something I need to talk to you about.'

'Yes.' Bel flopped down onto the bed, and Joe sat down next to her, handing her the cup of herbal tea.

'Hey. Married, eh?' He nudged her shoulder with his and she smiled.

'Married. I can't wait, Joe.'

He chuckled. 'Me neither. Your dad wants to give us a present.'

'He does? But they've already given us all that beautiful crockery.'

'Something more. He said that one day we might want to move back to London.'

Bel puffed out a breath. 'But we love this house! And… London?' Joe had made his peace with London, but it was still the place he'd left to make a new life.

'London's a good place to live. And when the baby comes…'

'He knows about the baby?' Bel's hand moved protectively to her tummy.

'No, and I didn't tell him. But wouldn't you like to be nearer to your mum? Just a few streets away, maybe? A house that's a bit smaller than your mum and dad's, and needs some work? Think of all the shopping trips with your mum, while your dad and I babysit.'

That would be… Bel wasn't going to even think about it, it would so easily turn into a dream for the future.

'Do you really want that, Joe? Our home is here, isn't it?'

'My home is with you and our baby, Isabella. We'd have to keep this house, because we'll need somewhere to stay when we come back to Rome. I don't want to give the clinic up, or our plans to expand and open a few more, and there will still be grapes to pick in the garden and improvements to make…' Joe's smile made it all sound so tempting.

'Stop it, Joe. You're all I need, and this last eighteen months…you've made me so happy.'

'You've made *me* happy. Now that we know what we can do for ourselves, maybe it's time to widen our horizons a bit. When I was offered that teaching post back in London, they said that they understood I had commitments here, and that their offer was open-ended. And maybe it's time for you to start talking with your dad about the trust again.'

'But…' Bel heaved a sigh. 'Can we risk it? When we already have so much more than we'd ever thought possible.'

He took her hand, his thumb straying to the love knot on her finger. That had never been replaced, and never would be. 'Remember all of those promises we made to each other? We've kept them, and we've grown into the life that we wanted. I think it's time to do more now, because we both have more to do. You want to vote on it?'

Bel chuckled. 'I love you so much, Joe. My vote's for London.'

'Mine is too. We don't need a tie-break, but just out of interest…'

'The baby's going to love London too. And our house here in Italy.'

He grinned at her. 'Looks like it's unanimous. You want to tell your dad that we're accepting his offer, or shall I?'

'We'll tell him together.' Today was meant to be the day for them to cement all of their dreams. But suddenly there were new dreams as well.

Chiara had joined her mother, helping with the long row of tiny buttons at the back of Bel's wedding dress. Uncle Edo had done her proud with a simple knee-length creation, textured with white embroidery on the bodice and cuffs, which Chiara had helped to design and stitch.

The assembly room at the local town hall was full to the brim with family and friends, along with staff and patients from the clinic. As Bel and her mother entered she saw Joe and her father both jump to their feet, and a murmur of excitement ran around the guests. The bridal march started to play, and Bel squeezed her mother's hand. 'Ready, Mum?'

'Are *you* ready?'

Joe was waiting for her, the smile on his face the only thing that she could see. Bel was more ready than she'd ever been for anything. She started forward, her mother hurrying to catch up with her.

And then...it was like a series of wedding photographs, all taken through the lens of her own eyes and engraved on her mind. The way Joe spoke his vows, loud and clear for everyone to hear, although the look on his face told Bel that they were for her alone. Her dad hugging his new son-in-law and shaking his hand. Her mother's scream of delight when they told her that they'd be seeing her in London after the honeymoon, to take a look at a new house. The blizzard of confetti and the open fire outside the village hall, which beckoned the guests in to the feast that her parents had organised. Dancing and laughter and, most of all, the love that shone in Joe's eyes.

Then it was time to go. Joe helped her into the white woollen coat that Uncle Edo had made to go with her dress and keep her warm on their journey. A good half of the guests had decided to accompany the wedding party in seeing them off, while the other half stayed behind to keep the party going for their fellow guests' return. Joe helped Bel into the back seat of their car and Chiara's husband drove them to the assembly point, taking the car on to the spot they'd agreed on, a few kilometres along the road.

They stood together on the cobbles of the Via Appia. Lanterns were lit in the gathering dusk and her parents presented one to each of them, to light their way. A cheer went up as Joe kissed her.

'It's a long road, Isabella.'

'The longer the better. We'll walk it together.'

'Always.' He kissed her again, prompting another cheer.

Other walkers and cyclists had stopped to watch, and as Bel took Joe's arm and they started to walk the sound of wild applause followed them.

Their gazes were already set on the shadowed shape of the horizon up ahead. 'Our first steps, Isabella,' Joe murmured. 'Do you know how much I love you?'

'Yes, I do.' He'd never left her in any doubt of it, and come what may he told her every day about all that was in his heart. 'Do you know how much I love you, Joe?'

'I feel it every day.'

An evening star rose in the sky as they walked. Setting off on a journey that so many had made along this road. One that would last them a lifetime.

* * * * *